THE NEGATIVE CUTTER

Patrick Chapman

The Negative Cutter

two stories

The Negative Cutter

is published in 2014 by
ARLEN HOUSE
42 Grange Abbey Road
Baldoyle
Dublin 13
Ireland
Phone/Fax: 353 86 8207617
Email: arlenhouse@gmail.com
arlenhouse.blogspot.com

Distributed internationally by
SYRACUSE UNIVERSITY PRESS
621 Skytop Road, Suite 110
Syracuse, NY 13244–5290
Phone: 315–443–5534/Fax: 315–443–5545
Email: supress@syr.edu

978–1–85132–089–9, paperback

Typesetting by Arlen House

Cover image by Sean Hayes
'Detritus Series 2', photograph, 2012
http://seanski50.wordpress.com/type/gallery/

Contents

For Sara

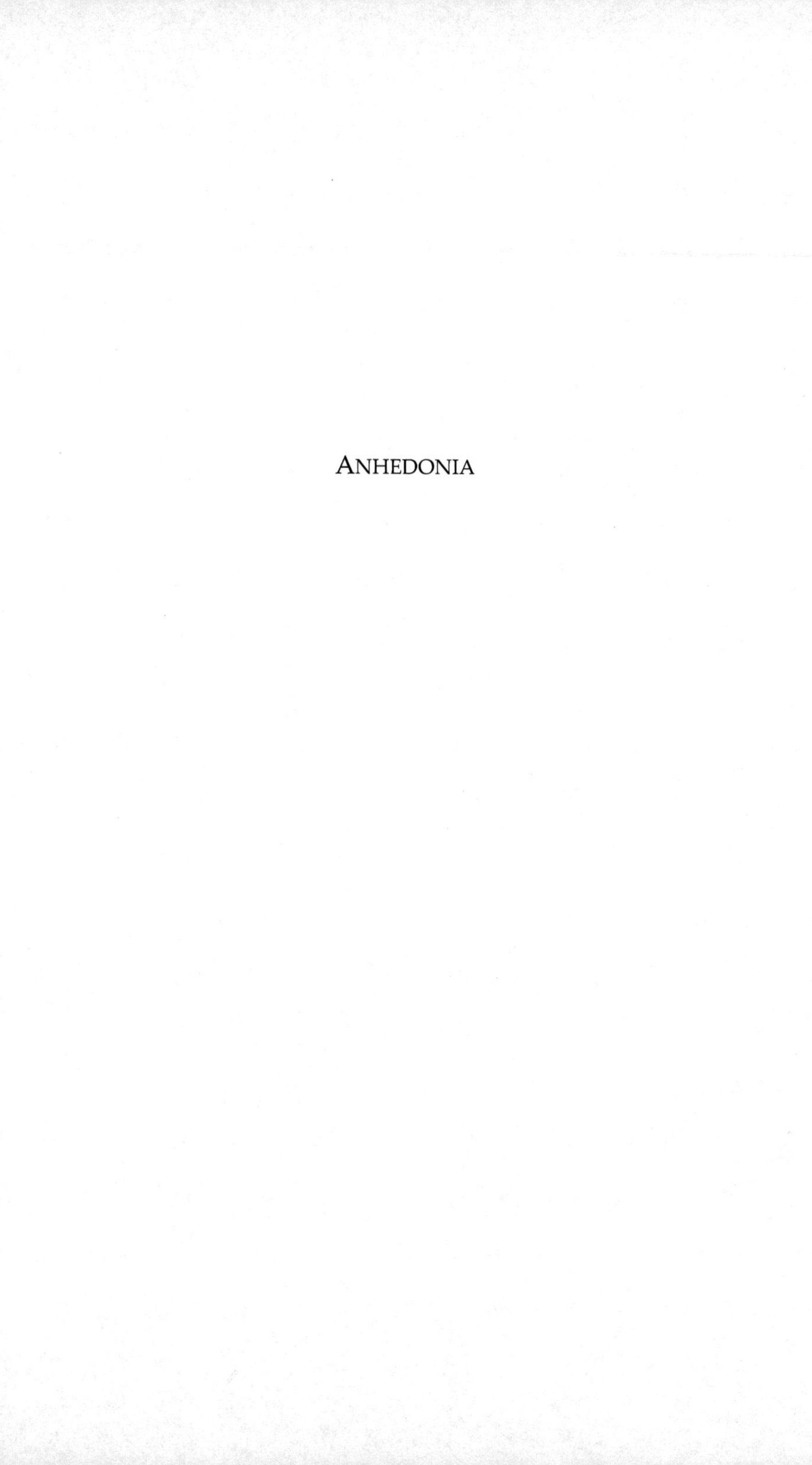

ANHEDONIA

I

The social committee at Ampersand Bailey Ampersand had chosen a Wild West theme for the agency's client Christmas party. This was now entering its third hour in a function room of the Bush Hotel, a marketing-driven venue that, according to its literature, prided itself on being luxurious and efficient. The hotel's owners failed to understand that you could not truly be both at the same time. Tony Bright knew, because he had written the literature in question and had objected to that wording but was overruled. He imagined that she knew too – Dora Potts, a striking brunette who worked in the accounts department of the biscuit company for whom &B& created the advertising. She was out there in the crowd and he didn't think he was in with a shout. There were too many well-adjusted cowboys between him and her.

That winter Garth Brooks and his ilk were in their pomp. Tony thought of the singer as 'Garth Vader'. Twice that night in reference to this, and quite pleased with himself, he had said to one colleague or another, 'I find your lack of taste disturbing'. Neither had got the reference, leaving him feeling like a walking *non sequitur*.

No one in the room would get that either if he said it, so he didn't.

The DJ persisted in playing more mellow country rock than was good for Tony's teeth and now another bout of line dancing had just broken out in a sudden, unstable grid. From the table where he sat alone, Tony watched the dancers with something approaching appalled anthropological fascination, mingled with dread that anyone would ask him to hit the floor for a closer look at this phenomenon, let alone to take part. He had tried to be casual all night. Indeed his only concession to the evening's theme was the white cowboy hat he wore with his black suit; this made him look like the caterer at a funeral in *Dallas* rather than the man with no name. Tony preferred to let others do the peacock stuff while he skulked quite unmolested in the shadows, smiling up every now and then at a passing account handler, or avoiding the gaze of Katee the media buyer, whom he had snogged two Christmases before while his judgment had been slightly impaired by punch, vodka, brandy, red wine, mulled wine, limoncello, Guinness, gin and something Swiss with gold flakes floating in it and 'shlag' in the name. Tonight he had not been drinking quite as much and felt the worse for it, though he wouldn't need an ambulance this time. Alcohol, he found, could be like that sometimes.

Dora, got up as a Red Indian of the Disney nation, line danced as part of a waffle of temporary cowpokettes to "Achy Breaky Heart", Billy Ray Cyrus's crowning achievement to date. She spotted Tony and made eye contact, catching his attention with her wonky gaze and curious smile. He appraised her looks, found them stimulating and immediately dismissed his chances, no matter that she was the one who had sent the first smoke signal. Still, he liked the cut of her: petite, elfin and with a black bob. She was absolutely one of his types, all of which he had categorised as 'Unattainable Type No 1', 'Unattainable Type No. 2', and so on. With her war paint, tan suede outfit, moccasins, headband and feather, she looked like a movie star of the 1930s. She was therefore, being made of celluloid, impossible to have sex with. That was how he liked it. It meant that he did not have to actually consider going over and talking to her. Rejection, when it came, inevitable though unprovoked, would not carry as much of a sting.

Dora saved him the effort. She broke formation, strode purposefully over to her table, picked up her drinks – she had three, all differently-coloured – and made a beeline to where Tony was hiding out. With more of the appalled fascination he had experienced earlier in general and was experiencing now in particular, he watched her very swiftly put the drinks down on his table and, without an introduction, jump into his lap and fling her arms around his neck. His chair collapsed under their combined weight and they found themselves rolling on the floor, unexpectedly laughing their heads off before a word had been said. It was the best chat-up line he would ever hear in his life. Within seconds, though Tony did not find out about this until the following morning, he and Dora were an item.

Waking up in his flat he saw that the girlfriend fairy had been and had left something nice.

'Howdy, Calamity Dora', Tony stirred in the bed and attempted a levity for which it was too early in the day. 'Or was that Little Squaw Drinky-Something-Bleh'. His words trailed into mumbles and a burp.

Luckily for Dora, she was still not quite awake and was doing that thing Tony found cute in women, that moistening of the dry roof of the mouth, then lip-licking while squeezing eyes closed and making a little moan of not wanting to get out of bed, a 'mnmn' that he adored instantly. She sounded like a warm duvet felt. Women, he told himself, are lovely. This one takes the prize as the loveliest thing in Lovelytown. Despite the ugly hangover squatting in his head, he made a mental note to write to Billy Ray Cyrus, thanking him for recording such an appalling tune that Dora had been left with no choice but to abandon the dance floor at that exact moment the previous night.

Outside it was a bright Saturday morning in winter. Snow fell gently, birds sang something in German, probably by Beethoven, and a clear, crisp, frosty breeze conferred a magical freshness on the air that wafted in through the open window of the bedroom. Tony noticed none of it. He didn't even consider why they had left a window open in winter. He was busy watching Dora sleep, and wondering how on earth he had managed to convince her to come home with him.

Naked and close in bed one night at her place, warm and wrapped in each other's breathing, Dora and Tony connected from their ankles to their necks like batteries about to power up the room. He felt comfort in her scent, a trace of some perfume he could not name. It made him think of a garden in Tahiti.

With the volume low they listened to Maxi on the radio. Dora's bedside double-cassette mini-system had a piece of masking tape with the word 'No!' in bold blue biro on it, placed over the deck that did not work. The minute he first saw this, and even now after three weeks, Tony found it adorable.

'Adorable' – this popped into his head – wrapped his girlfriend's name inside the word 'able'. That must mean something. He could not think of a word that embraced his own name satisfactorily. 'Antonym' didn't cut it.

'Monotony' failed to bookend the name. Tonight, in Dora's arms, his mind wandered around such pleasing thoughts. In the morning he would have to buy a thesaurus.

Now Maxi played Ella Fitzgerald performing "Let's Fall in Love" from the Songbook. He had always liked that album but had lent his copy so long ago that he'd forgotten to whom.

Dora sang gently along with the melody then stopped and looked him in the eye. 'Are you an educated flea?' she purred. 'Let's do it!'

They made a start and things went quite well until Maxi followed Cole Porter with the theme from *Mission: Impossible*. Tony and Dora drew away from each other laughing, before gently recombining in a successful attempt to prove the song title wrong.

Many were the small but genuine domestic pleasures they shared. Tony especially enjoyed her kitchen. He liked preparing a meal for two while Dora put on a Shangri-Las tape and set the table; or amused him with the latest exploits of her younger sister Mary's deadbeat husband Kevin; or sneaked up behind him at the sink to slip her arms around his waist and squeeze.

One particular evening seemed to stand in his memory for all of them. With nothing to do while they waited for dinner to cook, Dora pulled off his shirt to get at his nipples and raise them with her tongue. Then she led him into the bedroom. In the twenty-five minutes before the oven timer went off, they made love in a delicious, slow and tender merging of their bodies. His was a lost cause, uncared-for and out of shape. Hers remained petite with a little pot-belly that he loved to stroke. Dressing, they talked about her becoming a belly dancer, and joked about him doing the same.

Back in the kitchen she set the table, lit a pair of candles, tuned the radio to Dave Fanning's show and poured the wine that he had opened an hour earlier to let it breathe.

Days like this, Tony got an education in alternative rock music and domestic bliss. They would take their time over eating and talk of whatever concerned them that day: her thesis in Marketing, which she was studying part-time; his latest campaign for something new and fantastic and beige; their plans for the weekend.

Evenings were filled with music as well: My Bloody Valentine, with their inverted architecture; Radiohead, whose song "Creep" Dora loved; girl-groups of the 1960s. Elvis Presley's "Crawfish" made her laugh bawdily. The Sneaker Pimps' "How Do" once set off a conversation about Britt Ekland's bottom-double in *The Wicker Man*. Tony suggested that marriage was like the plot of that film. One of the parties was destined to end up on fire in a cage constructed to reflect the other's view of the world. Dora said she hoped he was joking.

After Laurie Anderson's *Nerve Bible* show at the National Concert Hall, they agreed that from then on they would speak only in monosyllables, as in the beat of "O Superman", but Tony called out 'Taxi!' and put paid to that.

Some nights, they simply lay on their bellies on the carpet in his flat or hers and watched a film. Because she had seen a lot of television growing up, Dora knew everything about every movie ever made, it seemed. She filled many a gap in his cinematic education. *Singin' In The Rain* was one of her favourites: 'I cayan't stayand it!' If it had Audrey Hepburn in it, she knew the lines. If it had Cary Grant in front of the camera or Hitchcock behind it, and especially if it had both, she loved it. If Carmen Miranda sang in it, Dora knew the lyrics. Shirley MacLaine was one of her favourite actresses. Watching *The Apartment*, Dora asked, 'Will we ever get our own place?'

'Maybe', Tony said.

'It's just that I think things are going really well and you're adorable and it'd be brilliant, so there'.

'Maybe'.

'I love you', Dora said. 'That's one good reason for shacking up, baby'.

'Let's talk about it later, Dora'.

'All right'. Dora was disappointed but did not let it show. He could become suddenly and inexplicably irritable but it was other people, as far as he was concerned, who were difficult. Tony would change; she could handle his moods. They were worth it for the rest of him.

Washing up one summer evening after a stir-fry, a bottle of sake and *Annie Hall*, Tony broke his wedding-ring finger. A plate slid from the draining board into the sink and because of his lightning reflexes he reached out to catch it but instead cracked his hand on the edge of the sink. His arm was in a sling for a week. In the evenings Dora took pleasure in exaggerating the extent of his injury so that she could look after him. At work she told one colleague that he had been fisting her. Tony would have been shocked to hear her say such a thing so she didn't mention it to him.

He was becoming prone to accidents, it seemed. A month after the sling came off he caught a cactus plant as it fell from the windowsill in his living room. Nurse Dora made a poultice by soaking white bread in boiling water. She applied it to his fingers and later used tweezers to remove the spines.

'I'll take care of those, babe', she said. 'You poor little porcupine'.

Weeks later it was Dora's turn. In the early hours of a Thursday when Tony wasn't even there, she got out of bed to go to the loo in the dark. On the way back she banged into the bedroom door and gave herself an aubergine shiner. She wore sunglasses to work the next day. The girls in the office were inquisitive of course. That night Tony was not remotely surprised when Dora told him of their first assumption.

Tony was rubbish at cards but Dora indulged him and played. Believing that his victories had to be earned, she never let him win just to be kind. Now after a game of gin rummy, they lay on a blanket in his living room, watching "José Chung's *From Outer Space*". Wine glasses stood on the carpet beside the ashtray, their cigarettes and a half-empty Bin 45, which was the poshest bottle Tony could find in the corner shop.

They toyed idly with each other's bodies, his hand on the small of her back under her pink twinset cardigan. Her right ankle was crossed over his left. They might discover the secret of fire by rubbing them together.

'This is lovely', Dora said. 'Hey, can I use your 'puter to type up my essay?'

That very second, blue lightning flashed, exposing the bare trees outside like the bones of the sky. Tony rolled away from her and turned the television off for safety then rolled back. Dora called out 'Heyulp!' like Penelope Pitstop. He loved her for that.

Soon they were crouching under the window in mock fear and real awe at the power of nature. They clung together, daring the lightning to singe their extremities as they pulled each other's clothes off and fucked. This one, Dora remarked later, was definitely a 'fuck'. After the lightning they made a pot of tea and sat in the dark, drinking it.

'The richness of the ordinary, illuminated by forks of electricity', Tony said.

Winter came and went. Spring had only just turned up when summer grabbed its seat, to keep it warm for autumn.

Dora, one Saturday in August in Delight, their favourite café: 'I am the fast one you pulled'.

Dora also, on Merrion Square as they walked past the American College: 'That's where they teach you how to walk and chew gum'.

Tony, in Stephen's Green, feeding swans with Dora's bread: 'Pigeons. Hmm. Pigeons with notions'.

September brought them away for a week to a place that for them felt exotic. In the bookshop of the Uffizi, Dora absentmindedly took the hand of a total stranger, thinking it was Tony beside her. She discovered her mistake when the young man coughed with embarrassment, said '*Entschuldigung*', and let go. Dora laughed in mortification.

That night in the hotel, she cited the incident as her excuse to kiss Tony from the tips of his toes to the crown of his head. She took her time, covering every inch, rediscovering in particular the sensitivity of his hips. Then she turned him over and started on the other side and when she had finished, they agreed that her debt had been overpaid and he owed her a refund. He would have to lick her all over, the very next night. That started a series of retaliatory sexual acts over the following weeks that brought them close to melting into each other, never to find their individual selves again, or so he thought.

At the end of July, they spent a week house-sitting in an apartment overlooking Dame Street. It belonged to Mary, who had gone away on a business trip while her husband took the opportunity to visit his elderly parents in Dundalk. Dora and Tony found that they enjoyed this taste of togetherness. They had brought with them changes of clothes, and enough CDs so that they would not have to play the Bryan Adams records her sister favoured, or the Iron Maiden discs of her husband. They had brought books and food and a crate of wine. For a whole week the place was theirs. It was a thrill to have a flat in the centre of town for a change. Work for both of them was now a short walk away. Tony enjoyed coming home to her, knowing that she was also coming home to him. Something felt right about it. He liked this pad.

'That husband', Tony said one morning in the bathroom while she brushed. 'He can't be too much of a deadbeat if he's got a place like this'.

'They've got a place like this', Dora corrected him. 'Mary pays most of the mortgage. Kev's a platinum slacker with a degree in laziness from the university of "duh"'.

'He works in a bookshop', Tony said. He stepped into the shower.

On the Friday they chose to spend the time with each other rather than joining their respective work crews in the pub. After dinner they took a bottle of Romanian red and sat on a bench in the roof garden, looking out over the city. Tony lit up a cigarette.

'That's a fierce view', he said. 'I think I'd like to live in a bustly kind of place'.

Dora had a suggestion. 'Let's go to San Francisco then. Let's live there! You me and the Golden Gate Bridge'.

'Let's try it out first to see if they'll let us in'. Tony flicked some ash on the patio. 'You never know with America. Bill Clinton might kick us out'.

'Clinton isn't the type to kick anyone out, especially not for eating crisps'. Dora beamed delight at her boyfriend. 'I want crisps'.

Saturday, they booked flights at a travel agent on Dawson Street and when they came out, Tony with the tickets in his hand, Dora made him promise that they would not once, not ever, sing Scott McKenzie.

Having tramped up creaking stairs to the second floor of a noodle bar in Chinatown for lunch, they sat by a door that opened wide on empty space.

'There are no other customers', Tony said. 'Is that bad?'

'Who has a step big enough to walk in off the street?' Dora almost smiled.

'Who puts a door there?' Tony asked.

The old lady who brought the food mocked Dora's chopstick technique, or so it looked to Dora, but perhaps the woman was only being helpful. Tony noted her frown and he looked over at the woman, who didn't see him.

Tony sighed. 'That woman was rude. I'm sorry, babe'.

'It was just her way'.

'The Chinese way'.

'Now you're being racialist'. Dora put her chopsticks down. 'One of these days you'll make a remark and take someone's eye out'.

Aimless wandering restored their calm. Dora spotted a restaurant that had only rabbit on the menu. 'Wabbit season', she said. 'Let's never go there'.

It was a truism that seeing these buildings for the first time not on television, made the world seem both bigger and smaller. Soon Dora and Tony were agreeably lost in the strange familiarity of the place.

'This whole town is a rollercoaster on pause', Dora said.

At the foot of Columbus Avenue, Tony gawked up at the TransAmerica Pyramid. Dora admired the Sentinel Building squatting in front of them. They spotted Vesuvio across the road.

'I couldn't swear to it', Tony said, 'but isn't this corner where Chekov asks about the nuclear wessels?'

'What?'

'*Star Trek IV*'.

Five minutes later they were perched at a table on the first floor of Vesuvio and had ordered straight bourbons.

'We're upstairs again', Dora said. She took out her *Rough Guide* while Tony studied the mural in Jack Kerouac Alley. Dora looked up from her book. 'You know this bar opens twenty-three hours a day? It's like an inverted prison cell'.

'Look', he said, indicating City Lights. 'There's where the beats used to drink'.

'I think you'll find that's a bookshop', Dora said. 'The sign sort of gives it away. And they probably didn't do booze. Just black coffee and drugs and sodomy'.

Five hours later they stumbled out into the illuminated street and could not remember where they had put their goddamn hotel.

Despite his somersaulting hangover Tony wanted to see the U.S.S. *Pampanito* at Fisherman's Wharf. In their hotel room that morning Dora was not so sure that a water-based vehicle was really the best place to find herself, given that she already had the bends from all of the bourbon they had taken on the night before. Tony convinced her. He really wanted to see what it was like to be in an actual, real submarine and Dora admitted that she was curious. She made him promise that they would go to Sam Woh's for lunch afterwards, then on to the Castro. Tony agreed. 'You can find out just how curious you are', he said.

On board the *Pampanito* they found it easier than expected to walk the narrow passage along its length though once or twice Tony felt the walls closing in on him.

'So much machinery, so little explanation', he said. The explanations were there but he did not look for them. Everything was painted glossy grey, which added to his feeling of oppression. The bunks were barely big enough for one; the crew rooms were tiny. 'How did all these men live in this cramped space?'

'It's very intimate', Dora agreed.

'It mustn't have been fun to be a fat man on board', Tony joked.

Dora stopped walking, and touched him on the shoulder. 'Do you think I'm fat?'

He had never heard her ask that before. It didn't seem the kind of thing she would worry about. Dora took his silence as confirmation.

'You *do* think I'm fat'.

'Of course not!' Gently he took her hand off his shoulder and pulled it down around his waist so that they might embrace but he felt her resist.

'Are you afraid of being submerged, Tone?'

Another couple pushed past them. Backpackers who had insisted on bringing their luggage with them, these people were not, Tony observed, overly polite. He and Dora were forced to move aside and break their embrace. Then he almost lost his footing but she helped him up and as he righted himself he found a new sadness in her face.

'Sometimes a cigar-shaped submarine is just a submarine', Tony said. 'I don't know what I mean by that'.

Dora frowned. 'Let's get out of here', she said. 'I need some air'.

Dora cracked open a mussel. Sam Woh's was famous, her guidebook said, and she wanted to try the seafood. Tony appeared to have recovered from the *Pampanito* incident. More importantly, as far as he was concerned, so had Dora. She seemed lighter now.

He watched her pull the dead creature out of its shell with a fork and place it in her mouth. Then she landed a new thought on him, one he had not entertained.

'All right'. Dora chewed. 'Let's move in together, if that's what you really want'.

'Sorry?' He almost choked on a mollusc.

'When we get back, you leave your flat and I leave mine, and we get a place of our own. Goodbye suburbia. Hello new flat in town. News just in: nobody's ever lived there but us'.

'Every place you can think of, someone has lived there before'.

'Yeah, but you haven't and I haven't. Not together'.

'Ok, let's do it then', he said, more to end the conversation than to agree.

It was a gloriously bright and cold winter's morning at breakfast in Dora's flat when she and Tony had the talk again. The granola was particularly gritty today, so he blamed that for his reaction when she brought the subject up. Wheat-and-fruit-induced psychosis, he told himself later.

'I've seen too many couples consumed by the needs of their children', he began. Even as he spoke, Tony knew that he was making an excuse. 'There's this fellow at work says once you have them, your life is over. He and his wife are living for their kids now. All they ever talk to each other about are the little ankle-biters. The puke and the screaming and all that stuff they don't tell you about in

Romance School. He used to want to do music but she said she stamps very firmly on that kind of thing. Poor guy donated his Telecaster to Oxfam and became an account executive'.

'What if he wasn't talented and needed an excuse to save face?' she said. 'But this is us we're talking about'.

'He and his wife are always exhausted. They don't have sex any more'.

'For them the trade-off might be worth it. Don't you think it's worth it?'

'She has a wobbly belly', he said. 'Her tits are in her lungs'.

'Tone! You're a pig!'

It was true, Tony conceded, that some people found redemption in their kids but all he could see were the desiccated eyes, the premature baldness, the middle-aged spreads. These used-up specimens were the human equivalent of flowers that lose their lustre once they've released their pollen. To Tony, make-up looked weird on old women; and married men hobbled around, embalmed before their time. Nature was not our friend. It had no use for beauty once beauty had fulfilled its function. Everything had a function. The human body was merely a place for genes to crash while they prepared to move on.

'Freedom's relative', Dora said after a long silence. 'I love you but I also want babies. At least a couple of football teams' worth, like Mia Farrow, but not adopted from Vancouver or wherever'.

'That's Vietnam or possibly Korea. I think there's a supermarket where you get them. Asian Babies, five for a pound'.

'Why can't we do this? We have a nice thing here, babe. You're my man and I want it to be you'.

'Everything turns to shit in the end', Tony said and even the sound of his own voice brought him down.

'Oh god. Come here and give me a hug'.

Tony hugged her but not warmly. 'Don't worry, I'm fine'.

He considered himself a romantic but a failed one. He had seen his parents' marriage descend into a slow death of politeness and avoidance and religion, and he did not want the same for himself. Still he indulged Dora's aspiration to future happiness as long as she did not ask him to commit to it.

'Don't you want us to be old together, you and me, out on some porch in the desert, readin' in the sun, shootin' critters, sippin' whiskey?'

'Definitely maybe'.

Occasionally, Dora sheepishly admitted to having forgotten to take her Mercilon. When that happened, Tony would wait with dread for, as she put it, 'the redcoats to ravage her lady-garden'.

Dora's period didn't turn up. Just like that, one day her period didn't turn up. It didn't even phone ahead to say it would be delayed. She hadn't forgotten to take the pill. This thing had just happened. Sometimes it just happened. And she wanted to be sure, not to alarm him, so she waited a week to mention it.

'I'm late', she said at breakfast on the seventh day.

'But it's only twenty to eight'.

'No, I'm *late*'.

Tony stopped chewing his croissant. Dora had been short with him for days. Now he knew why.

'Oh, Dora'.

'I popped a morning-after pill as soon as I could get to a GP, but doesn't seem to have worked'.

On the way to work they stopped by a pharmacy and bought a pregnancy test. Dora promised him that she would wait to take it until they met at his flat after work.

Nine hours later, Tony paced the living room. Dora sloped off to the toilet with the white pen. When she came out, he knew by her face. A nuclear button had been pushed in the nuclei of cells.

Dora held the pen up for him to see. The blue lines in the window indicated the unthinkable. She burst into tears and dissolved in his arms. Tony held her for a long time then released her, took the test-pen from her grip.

'We should probably keep this for posterity'. He put the pen on the table.

Dora didn't hear him. She wandered away and collapsed on the sofa.

'I'll go get some booze', Tony said. Dora nodded assent.

He went out but as he was closing the front door he felt guilty for leaving her alone, even for a few minutes.

In the wine shop he bought two very posh-looking reds.

Dora was still on the sofa, appearing subdued, when Tony returned. He put the wine in the kitchen and went over to sit with her.

'I don't know what I want to do yet', Dora said. 'But whatever it is, I can't tell Mary. Maybe I can tell Joyce'.

'Not your parents, that's for sure'.

'Definitely no fucking way'.

They polished off both bottles in two hours.

'You're my man and I love you', Dora said that night in bed. 'Whatever we do, it's together'.

'All right', Tony said.

They fucked grimly a while later, the booze like molten fat in their bellies. Dora needed the intimacy. Tony reasoned that they might as well be hanged for a sheep as for a lamb.

The next evening, they sat in a greasy spoon on Talbot Street, one they'd never usually enter. Shoppers passed the window, oblivious to this, the most important drama now playing out on planet Earth. Tony resented that these people were too busy to pay any attention to them then he was glad of it. The dance music in this horrible café was too loud. The coffee was watery. He was glad of these things too. The world deserved to be just a little bit rubbish right now.

He watched her expression. Dora had taken on a blankness that he had never seen in her before. A stranger looked at him with her eyes. 'I've an appointment at the Well Woman Centre. Come with?'

'Of course'.

She put her hand on his. 'I know this isn't going to be easy'.

'I can't have a baby'.

'Neither can I'.

'But you're a woman'.

'Stop it', Dora said, and withdrew her hand. 'I'm going to England'.

'Oh. Oh, *right*'.

'It sounds like the name of a firm of lawyers', Tony said but Dora didn't answer.

Dilation & Curettage. He had heard the term before but it had never registered. Now it was staring at him from a leaflet on the table beside them. There was something like static in the soft t sound in dilation and the hard one in curettage.

A woman whom Tony took to be a counsellor came over. 'Dora Potts?'

'Yes'.

Tony and Dora both stood up.

'Who is this?' the counsellor dismissed him with her eyes.

'My partner'. Dora tried to sound businesslike.

'What is he doing here?'

Tony stepped back a pace to let Dora stand in front of him. The counsellor might be right. What was he doing here? For one thing, he wasn't running. He had hoped for a warmer welcome. Was he not one of the good ones?

'He's with me'. Dora sounded faint.

'Well you follow me, dear'.

Dora grimaced, embarrassed on his behalf.

'Just sit yourself down here', the counsellor said. 'She'll be out in a while'.

Tony slumped down on the bench that ran along one wall of the room. Three women sat at the other end, idly flicking through booklets that he expected were all about the joys of cystitis, hormone replacement therapy, osteoporosis. Every so often he felt the receptionist looking at him as though he were about to steal a pen.

A different nurse or counsellor or case-worker came by. 'Are you here with somebody?'

'Yes. My girlfriend ...'

The nurse nodded and walked away. Tony didn't understand. All he could think about was Dora. He had no idea what she and the counsellor might be discussing. He had no grasp of the detail.

Tony stared at the receptionist. She ignored him now so he gazed around the room to find something to focus on. The receptionist tapped on a keyboard. There were three other women here, sitting on the bench, each absorbed in thought.

'I'm here for her', Tony whispered in a hollow breath then wanted to take it back in case the words would become visible on the opposite wall like an audio graffito.

He got up and helped himself to coffee. A poster beside the machine offered free smear tests. Another warned against the dangers of smoking. He took his coffee to the noticeboard and read the covers of the leaflets pinned to it. They were all about options, choices, belly-dancing classes.

Tony wished things were different; he wished that the male pill had not been killed, as he assumed, by Big Pharma. He could have taken chemical control over his own fertility. Now there was nothing to be done but accept whatever Dora decided. He had no autonomy here. Lately, any time they had made love he had seen himself as a worker ant. Thinking of that now sparked alien feelings of hopelessness that he found unexpected and unworthy. He sat and finished his coffee then put the cup down on the first leaflet he had seen. *Dilation & Curettage.*

After some time the door opened. Dora said goodbye to the counsellor. Tony raised himself wearily, ready to put his arms around her but she did not look at him except to indicate that they should leave. She was clutching a leaflet.

They stayed at the lavish Gloucester Square pad in which Dora's younger sister Joyce lived with her successful City husband, Grant.

In the pub on the first night, Tony kept quiet. He understood perfectly that this was not the ideal way to meet Joyce. At one point Dora went to the toilet and Grant popped off to the cigarette dispenser. Joyce took Tony into her confidence.

'If you do a runner on my sister, I will find you and I will perforate your cranium with a bottle-opener. Got that? Also, your scrotum. Twice'.

He stared her out and she took his silence as assent.

'Good. We understand each other'.

Dora was returning from the loo. Joyce threw a faux-friendly smile at Tony, like she was discarding something mouldy for crows to pick over.

'How are we getting along?' Dora sounded medicated already.

Tony fixed on his pint and felt the sisters looking accusingly at him.

The next morning the taxi arrived at the flat. Joyce and Grant had both left for work, a fact for which Tony was grateful. He helped Dora with her night-bag down the stairs to the front door, and she fumbled with the spare keys that her sister had given to her.

The journey passed mostly without conversation. The driver took them to a clinic somewhere in north London.

On the way, Tony and Dora held hands. He wanted to make reassuring conversation but couldn't think what to say that would not upset her. He wanted to rattle on about Jim Carrey's new film or Blur's latest, or *Lois & Clark*. He wanted to make it all right but he had never felt so useless. Dora stared ahead.

The taxi dropped them off outside a building that might once have been a stately home, set in a cultivated garden surrounded by acres of woodland. Dora held tightly to her night-bag. Tony knew that it was full of girly things he didn't understand. He offered to carry the bag for her but she declined and he paid the driver. They walked towards the building.

Inside, at the reception area, Dora asked him to take a seat, so he did, and she went to check in. He looked around. The women here all wore dressing gowns. Tony assumed that most of them were Irish. When Dora came and sat beside him, he saw fear in her eyes. He squeezed her hand and said nothing. He did not know how long they waited until a nurse appeared in the corridor and gently called out *Dora Potts!* Tony told himself that Dora had just ordered a cut of meat in a deli and her number had come up – but he knew it couldn't have sounded that way. There was something wrong with his sense of hearing. They stood up and hugged tightly then Dora broke off and picked up her bag.

'See you tomorrow', she said and started to cry and he held her again but she kissed him on the lips and wiped her eyes and walked away.

The last thing he remembered before going to find a tube station was the sight of Dora and the nurse turning the corner into a room at the end of a pale green corridor.

On the way out the front door, he thought of her little toes poking out from under a medical gown, her lovely face at the other end, pale with dread. It killed him to wonder if he had put her here, if this was his fault; then he told himself that of course it was. Of course it was, and there was nothing he could do to help her, nothing at all.

For the rest of the day his mind took a vacation somewhere overcast and empty, in some North Korea of the brain. He must have done tourist things, gone to a cinema, even hit the Tate. For all he knew, he might have sat for hours in a Pret, or in several Prets, one after another. After the clinic, the other events of that day blackened in a fire of instant amnesia as soon as they occurred, leaving no traces but receipts and foreign lint in his pockets.

That weekend, before heading for the plane, Dora found in his luggage a copy of the Traveller's Companion edition of *The Naked Lunch*, from Henry Pordes on the Charing Cross Road. Tony had no recollection of buying it.

As requested, their taxi from Dublin airport took them to their separate homes. In the arrivals hall, Dora had asked

Tony for time alone, and said she would phone him when she was ready.

Four days later, they met in Delight, which Tony had stopped thinking of as their favourite café. It seemed to take forever to get their coffees, and the clattering of utensils, the chatter of other customers, the bossa nova on the radio, all conspired to fill the silence between them. When they sat down Tony tried small talk about work but it did not have any weight any more, this chit-chat.

Dora gazed at him gravely, expecting him to begin properly, to say something meaningful. It was all on him, he felt, but courage wasn't his bag right now. Courage was not where he had last left it.

'Are we ok?' Dora asked.

'I am if you are'. Tony drank some coffee and cursed the slurp he made.

'I need you', Dora said, 'now more than ever. I really need you now'.

'Why would you even consider staying with me?' He put down his coffee and the cup felt fragile in his hand.

'Tone, I need you'.

'Oh good', he said. 'Yes, yes, that's – I need you too'.

Now she smiled a little uncertainly but at least it was a smile.

For all his fear of the future, what really scared Tony was the thought of being without Dora. Now he knew that but not what to do about it.

He could not later remember how long it took for her period to start again. Dora told him at dinner in her flat. 'The redcoats are ravaging my lady-garden and I for one am mightily relieved'.

They were already sitting down or he would have grabbed her and hugged her like she had never been grabbed and hugged before. Instead, he merely put down his fork and briefly touched her hand.

'That is good news, I take it', he said.

Dora's gaze was solid, steady.

He returned it, imagining that their relationship was based now on a new maturity. They had come through. They had survived. Something had broken but something else had mended.

'You know I don't blame you, honey, for the recent events', Dora said. 'I want you to know that'.

'Thank you', Tony said. 'I did blame myself'.

'It was my choice'.

As time went on he came to know something else too. Dora was different. They both were. They might last a couple more years or they might go on forever.

So far they had continued to enjoy some of their old intimacy but everything, Tony felt, was tinged with a sadness that had become their common ground. Dora did not understand his silences but his dark moods were becoming less tolerable to himself now. He would sit for hours in silence, sometimes, not even watching whatever was on television. They didn't play gin rummy any more.

Tony awaited the fall of the hammer. She would find him out, he knew. She would see through his defences and find nothing inside and it would be all over, whatever it was that they had now. Dora might finally turn out to be 'Unattainable Type No 3'.

It was a year since San Francisco and time for their annual trip. Tired of adventure, they took an all-in deal and holidayed in Tunisia.

On the third day they followed the tour guide's advice and went on a bus trip into the desert. About three hours in, the driver told his passengers that this place they were driving through was 'where famous movie *Star Wars* was made'. Tony assumed that everywhere you went in this country was where the famous movie *Star Wars* was made.

Later the driver stopped at a Berber house, a sunken pit in which three generations of a family appeared to be on show as they sat, staring at the tourists who got out and walked around. There were eight others in the visiting party, and soon the house felt cramped. The numbers made Tony feel faintly embarrassed to be invading someone's home. By Dora's expression he could tell that she felt the same.

He stood apart and looked off into the distance, the endless desert. Dora came up beside him and took his shoulder.

'We're like the British meeting the natives', she said. 'It's a bit grim'.

'No', he said. 'It's worse than that. It's *Planet of the Apes,* and we're the apes'.

'They're getting paid to be gawped at'.

'You'd think, but I don't know'.

Hours later the bus stopped at El Jem. Their guide led them all underground to the cells of the amphitheatre. She explained that the slots in the roof had been designed to let the blood of dead Christians run in on the heads of their fellow lion-fodder.

'No wonder all those Christians are so barking', Tony said. 'I'd be mad if I had to work in those conditions'.

Dora snarked. 'Chip on your shoulder?'

At the desert hotel they and the others gathered in a traditional tent to dine on genuine Tunisian stews served from tagine pots. It seemed to be mostly lamb swimming in that wet couscous. A belly dancer turned up and Tony squirmed. He wouldn't know how to handle the attentions of another female in the presence of his girlfriend.

'She's very "volumptuous"', Dora observed.

Thankfully the belly dancer didn't make it to their table and Tony was glad when the mint tea arrived.

The following day after a too-early start, the driver brought them further into the desert for who knew how many miles, while the heat of the morning built into a baking front of air that drowsed them numb. In the afternoon the bus stopped. Tony and Dora stirred and looked out. They could hear voices and animal snorts. A group of camel herders waited for them. The driver and the guide ushered the tourists out of the bus.

Despite their laughing and cajoling Tony suspected these herders of not being actual simple traditional folk. They might have been Butlins crew for all he knew. It felt like a setup. At any moment, someone could attempt to sell them a piece of traditional tat.

The camel people hustled each tourist onto a beast, its head lowered to let the visitor climb up. The tour guide shouted general instructions into the air.

Tony checked that someone was attending to Dora, then he concentrated on his own ride. He put his right foot into a stirrup and slung his left over the camel's hump. Feeling queasy, he calmed his movements so that the camel would not sense his nervousness. He grabbed the reins with what he hoped came across as confidence. Someone yelled and the camels thundered off. Tony's teeth began to clatter and the coins in his shirt pocket jangled and fell away into the sand. He wanted to scream but wasn't sure if that was from fear or excitement.

He felt thunder between his legs and panic filled his breast. He shut his eyes tight then opened them again. Better to see what he was afraid of. He dug his thighs in to stop himself falling off then he relaxed and slowly began to trust his animal. He should let the camel drive.

It seemed to him that only minutes passed until their ride was at an end. The camels shuddered to a halt in front of a second gathering of local tribesmen, these ones holding tip jars and selling bottles of Coke. Did no one ever tell them that carbonated drinks were really not the thing for a desert thirst? Tony needed water. Somewhere in the distance, the tourist bus skidded at the head of a great wake of dust, turning to come and pick them up.

Tony's camel stopped beside Dora's. They glanced at each other, shaken and sore.

'That was freaky', she yelled over, 'but kind of fun'.

'That was freaky', Tony repeated. His camel bowed for him to dismount as Dora's did the same for her. She climbed off, her leg swinging across and down.

'My bum hurts', she said, her gait not what it was. A camel herder took the reins and led her animal away. Tony had climbed down now and the two of them hugged briefly before someone new came up to them and offered to sell them a drink. 'Coca-Cola! Coca-Cola! One dollar!'

It was a cool, red-streaked night. The bus arrived back at their tourist hotel and the guide asked everyone to applaud their driver. Soon they would be free of him, free of this bus. The driver unpacked the luggage from the hold and people took their things and dispersed into the hotel. Dora stomping behind him, Tony brought their bags straight up to the room.

He flopped onto the bed and Dora started to unpack in front of the dresser.

'Come here', he said. 'Leave that stuff'.

Dora continued unpacking. 'Girly stuff I need', she said.

Tony rolled on the bed, trying to create a comfortable niche for his back.

'You know, I don't think we've met an actual, genuine civilian Tunisian other than those involved in tourism', he said to the ceiling. 'And what about the political situation? Nobody's talked about it. Is it a democracy? A kingdom? I think we should be told'.

'Shush' Dora turned. 'I didn't know there was a political situation'.

'There's always a political situation'.

She held up one of his red-checked Burton shirts, crumpled. 'Look'.

Tony sat up and Dora showed him.

'For you', she said. 'I give you the desert'.

The breast pocket was full of Saharan sand. Tony took the shirt and folded it and kissed Dora on the nose.

'Now I'm stinky'. She began to undress for a shower.

An instrumental tune started up on the hotel radio. It was an extract from Mike Oldfield's *Amarok*. Tony secured the shirt by tying its arms and folding it over then bundled it into his suitcase.

'What's that weird music?' Dora asked before leaving the room.

'Don't know', Tony said. But he did know and wanted not to appear uncool, even to her, even after all they had done together.

He daydreamed for a while on the bed but as soon as Dora came out of the shower, her body wrapped in a towel, her hair still wet, he could not remember what he had seen.

Dora showed him her ring finger. 'When are you going to get me something to put on this? The girls at work are asking again'.

Dora's teasing inflection did not register. He fell back on the bed and let out a long, ungallant sigh.

The lesson Tony took from this moment seemed clear. If you are in a shaky relationship you should avoid going on package holidays.

The Olympia was heaving, so Tony and Dora stood at the back. Nick Cave prowled the stage. This theatre, with its air of seedy grandeur, suited him perfectly. The Bad Seeds were several songs in already and still hadn't done "Brompton Oratory". Tonight it wasn't that kind of gig.

Dora smiled over now at a man in the crowd. Tony recognised him as an actor he had once used in a radio commercial of the kind known in the business as 'Two C's in a K'.

'Is he your man from TV?' Dora asked.

Tony glared but he wasn't sure at whom. 'Which one?'

Cave's music throbbed dangerously on the air as if trying to have sex with it. The chords were not having any of this 'consent' nonsense and the atmosphere in here was getting sweaty, dirty despite itself. The atmosphere in here liked it.

'Your man'.

'He's a voiceover artist', Tony hissed. 'He does commercials during the day and a standup routine in the evening about the perils of selling out'.

'Hmm', Dora said, 'drinks?' She pushed through the crowd and no one seemed to mind. Tony followed. By the time they got to the bar, the actor had somehow contrived to be there too. The fucker was handsome, Tony thought, but not all that. He probably hadn't done a drama in years. Dora made eyes at the guy, who made eyes right back. Did those two know each other already?

Dora gave Tony the drinks to carry.

'What was that all about?' he asked.

'Nothing. Just looks familiar. Is he famous?'

Three songs went by but Tony didn't hear them. He finished his drink and dropped the plastic glass on the ground.

Dora went to the toilet and took her time. She returned with one of the security guards in tow, and was wearing a VIP bracelet. The security guard, barely tolerating Tony, grunted, 'Hold out your hand'.

Confused, Tony obeyed the guard, who slapped a bracelet on his wrist. The guard led them to the VIP enclosure in front of the stage. Dora jumped up and kissed the guard on the cheek. 'Thanks!' she chirruped and the big oaf lumbered away.

For three more songs, Dora stood with her back to Tony, who now hated Nick Cave and all who sailed in him. Tony couldn't see the band, though they were right there. Nick Cave's quiff was almost in his face. All Tony could see was Dora's back. Perspiration showed through her dress.

Just before the encore, the actor shoved into the VIP area and, as Tony watched, leaned into Dora. He shouted above the music into her ear, 'You're beautiful!'

Then with a flash of fuck-me dentistry, Dora yelled back. 'I know!'

Tony's stomach started to hurt. The actor melted into the crowd.

Dora looked back at her boyfriend, grabbed his hand and pulled him over to stand beside her, right there, as "Tupelo" started.

'How did you manage to wangle the VIP bracelets?' he yelled.

'I'm a beautiful woman, Tone', she shouted. 'I know how to use my mouth to get what I want!'

'Your mouth?' At first he couldn't think of anything else to say. What was happening to her? Then a retort occurred to him. 'What about feminism?'

'Feminism, schmeminism', Dora said, suddenly the Lady Captain of the Iron John golf team. 'Let's get a drink, hey!' She dragged him towards the bar like he was Samsonite but he backed away and she let him go.

"Tupelo" continued. Tony shoved through the crowd, across the beer-sticky floor to the exit and out into the art-deco lobby. He waited beside the T-shirt stand inside the front door to see if she would come out.

Dora didn't seem in a hurry. When she emerged, the look on her face begged a challenge.

Tony didn't move. He let her come to him. 'What was that all about?'

'You tell me!' she said.

'What do you mean, you tell me?'

'I'm going home. Alone. To my flat'.

'Shit, Dora –'

Now she stared like he was a stranger. Now she stood right in front of him and stared into his face. 'Oh, Tone. What was wrong with us?'

'I never led you on', he hissed. 'I never led you on'.

Where had that come from?

Then he saw it, an immense sadness in her eyes and a bitter smile as she shook her head. He couldn't bear it.

Dora punched him in the face. She turned on her heel and stormed out into the street past the bouncers, who glared back at Tony.

Hand cupped around his nose, he cursed her aim and thanked her for the pain and rushed out after her and imagined a taxi driver, blinded by her devastating beauty, crashing into the front of the Olympia while doing a U-turn just for her. Just to pick her up.

Dora didn't look back. She simply got smaller as she walked and didn't stop. She evaporated in the darkness as he watched and that was it, her final fade-out.

Early the next morning he married the duvet. He decided to never get out of bed again. Why was it always the normal people who went mad? But if Dora had been insane, he could have backed away with impunity. She was better adjusted than he could ever be. He loved her but he couldn't be with her, because he couldn't be with anyone and he didn't know why. All he felt was the ache of it.

From the descriptions in women's magazines as well as from the lyrics of Dora's Alanis Morissette tape, he knew himself to be an immature male. Something like that. There was definitely a name for what he was.

Over the weeks and months after Dora's departure, self-loathing became his philosophy. He knew that this would not get him anywhere but it was fine because there was nowhere he wanted to go ever again. Tony descended into calm despair and random drinking at home. He got fatter; he lost control. He wandered around in a haze of acute nothing. When there is nothing, there is no time, which therefore cannot heal.

In the following couple of years, Tony saw Dora twice in the street. On both occasions she turned her face and hurried past like he'd given her some kind of disease she had just managed to get rid of and was unwilling to contract again.

II

There are some things that, once you have done them with someone you love, you will never do as well on your own. So there were certain experiences Tony simply did not have any more. Nor did he fool himself into thinking that they were available to him; he knew that they required at least the peripheral involvement of someone else. As far as love was concerned, he was all out. Not only that, but there were gaps in his memory so that he could never be quite sure of what exactly he had lost.

Isolated moments returned to him from time to time. He experienced this as a kind of torture – fragments of a life he had thrown away. Some of those remnants came to him nowadays; some of those things he no longer did.

He did not go to the beach for a walk on a Sunday afternoon. He did not massage Dora's back with oil impregnated with *chypre*. He did not play Trivial Pursuit with his Dora, belly down on the carpet, drinking wine in front of a real fire. He did not wake up in the morning beside her, reach over and tease a response of delight from her skin. He did not carelessly flaunt his superior knowledge of inconsequential things. He did not arrive at the office in the morning incapable of keeping a grin from his face or a certain awkwardness from his gait. He did not have to go to the bathroom in the middle of the day because he had just got a hard-on while thinking about her. He did not spontaneously stop what he was doing because he felt compelled to call her. He did not do drugs because he did not like to take them alone. He did not sit in bed at night reading to her from *Black Dogs* or *The English Patient* or *My Secret Garden: Women's Sexual Fantasies*. He did not end up with her at parties by mistake and help her demolish a bottle of Absolut someone had left. He did not discuss his problems with his male friends because he did not have any male friends left; he had gradually withdrawn from the company of others and rarely saw anyone but the people at work. He did not dally in the off-licence wondering whether to go for the Michel Lynch or the Barolo, because it was her birthday. He did not play cards with her on a train, smoking in the smoking car, playing footsie under the table on their way to Kilkenny, or somewhere exotic for the weekend. He did not turn up at her office with a bunch of flowers for no particular reason, embarrassing her. He did not nurse her when she was ill. He did not revel in just strolling by the canal with her after a night in the pub. He did not accompany her to the doctor when she had women's trouble. He did not go to sleep at night, listening to the disc jockey recounting the names of saints whose anniversary it was. Two years after Dora left, and with nothing else to do, Tony decided to kill himself.

It was a pointless Sunday afternoon. Tony wallowed like a hippo in his bath, drinking cheap wine from Romania, replaying memories of Dora, concluding that he could either do something about her or accept that it was too late, that it was over. It had been forever, forever and five minutes at least. She had probably moved on. What was he holding on to?

The oil in the bath, a sharp citrus tang, he had dropped in like a tincture of some angel's sweat, and it reminded him of the woman lost too long ago now. Having chosen a kind of freedom, he discovered that he had never been as free as when he had belonged to someone else. His monkey-brain chattered with twisted stories, half-truths, outright lies.

The world was full of stories. Some were versions of real events but never the events themselves. Language was the carrier oil into which we dropped our scented recollections. Each time it was different.

He remembered a woman from college who had called her mother and said she wanted to move back from Chicago to Ballyvaughan, have babies and get married. On her return they drew up a list of eligible local men. The criteria were that he must be not be ugly, gay or poor. They made a shortlist of boys with whom she had been in school, men with whom she had once gone out and men who had earning potential. Then she set about ringing their numbers. 'Hi, this is Jo. I'm looking for – Oh, my God, is that – Séamus? Well isn't that – I haven't seen you in – That's fecking cool, ya shocker. What are you doing Thursday?'

Within a year she was married to Séamus. She told her city friends that her childhood sweetheart had waltzed back into her life and what was a girl to do? Her mother let the true story slip to Tony's mother, months later at a meeting of the Charismatic Renewal Movement. The groom was always kept in the dark and ignorance did indeed turn out to be bliss. Tony was not sure of the moral.

He considered what the difference was between this and picking someone up in a bar. You went through the same process of evaluation but on a different time scale and usually it didn't matter in the end how the match was made.

To him it seemed a similar process to buying soap. If you didn't like what this brand did for you, you would simply choose a different one next time. If you did like it, you might take home other items in the range.

Thinking that he might write a book on the subject, he began testing theories aloud, his voice, on account of the wine, more unlovely than usual. In his head he sounded like Woody Allen at the beginning of *Manhattan*.

'Chapter One. Love is the name we give to our potential for disaster. It is the reason we allow ourselves to offer hostages to fortune. When a man and a woman have a child, they look after it if they are decent. They protect it against hunger, terror and pain. Children are the hold the world has on us. They are our weakness and our strength, our human shields, the reason we knuckle down and endure totalitarian rule, a demeaning job, or a sudden tendency in our partners to religion. Children are why we adapt to whatever life throws at us. But the road we take, a diversion from all others, is signposted with exits we can't go down.

'This was my major departure from Dora. She found her path and I could only see a field. Hmm. Too philosophical'.

Watching the bubbles bursting around his body, he drunkenly remembered something else.

'Chapter Two. Why did my mother never have any more kids after me? There were the growths in her womb. That's gross. Could they have been psychosomatic? I can't even begin to guess at her unhappiness, wrapped in silence, but I know it's there. The tragedy is that Mum and Dad are of a generation that didn't believe in breaking up.

'Too maudlin'.

There in the bath, about to commit suicide, Tony recalled his first near-death experience, an accident involving a haircut and a car when he was four. His mother led him by the hand down the town to the shop with the red-striped pole outside, its big window showing off the one chair at which the barber did his work. He saw this strange man and what he was doing to the head of the customer in the chair, removing parts of his victim and letting them fall to the floor. Terrified, little Tony tore loose from his mother's grip and ran out into the traffic. A passing Hillman Hunter nearly knocked him dead, but his mum ran out and yanked him to safety in time. Screaming, she whacked him across the head for having frightened the life out of her. Then she took him up tenderly in her arms and carried him in. Crying his eyes out, confused as hell and still shitless, Tony endured his first professional haircut on a head throbbing with the pain of a blow from the mother who loved him.

When they were about five, he and his boyhood friend Mervyn sat beside each other in the classroom, sharing a roll of Love Hearts while the teacher tried to show the children what the colour blue was.

'It's the sky'.

Mervyn took one out of the roll and gave it to Tony. It said 'I Love You'. Tony grabbed it and ate it. The next one in the roll said 'Buzz Off'. Tony picked that out and handed it to Mervyn, who took offence and moved his seat away, then dropped the Love Heart to the floor. For the rest of the class Tony thought about killing himself. He imagined holding his stupid head in a lake until the water separated him from his shame.

'It's the colour of a bluebird'.

In the pub with his parents about a year after the Love Hearts Incident, young Tony saw a packet of Hermesetas that someone had left on a ledge. Thinking them to be pills that could finish him off, he stole the box and took an overdose of the sweeteners. He didn't die, and nobody even noticed his attempt. How long had he been thinking about this now and no one had picked up on it? Tony spent the next hour alternately staring up at *Van Der Valk* on TV, and observing his parents and their friends as they got drunker and drunker. He did not know that this was what they were getting. He did not even understand that this was something he did not understand. He was just there, suspended without supervision, with no feelings that he could name. When would those pills work? He waited and waited and nothing happened. Soon it was closing time.

And now it was another kind of closing time. Time to put memories away. What would his family think if he killed himself? But he wouldn't have to live with that.

He reached over to the tap end and got the bath bomb he'd left there. It made a fizz when he dropped it in the water then it exploded with a sherbet rush, releasing rose petals that covered the surface of the water like mutated lily pads for some amorous miniature frog. Under the harsh bathroom light, the petals glowed a vivid red as though infused with blood.

Here he was, full of wine and bullshit, of self-pity and remorse. Here he was, blaming himself for everything, for failing Dora in every way, for failing himself. Tony got tearful as only the Irish can, and wondered what he was going to do with his fuck-up of a life. But hadn't he figured that one out already? Over the course of two bottles of wine, the last glass of which he now finished in this bath, Tony determined that what he would do with his fuck-up of a life was this: he would end it.

He had earlier placed on the cistern a scalpel stolen from the finished-art stores at work. He stood up in the bath, put his glass down and reached for the scalpel like a

Roman nobleman or a Mafia soldier. On the oily surface of the bath, his feet slipped. He tumbled sideways and fell over, toppled out of the tub and slammed into the ground, the scalpel falling under him.

He landed on the floor, crumpling on the tiles in a twisted analogue of a human body that deserved to have a chalk line drawn around it. He banged his head and hoped that the concussion would at the very least start a gush of internal bleeding.

'Goodbye, Dora', he mumbled in that final moment.

He cried some more and entered a kind of dreaming in which he heard snatches of talk from the past.

'I never led you on. I never led you on'.

'I tore her heart in two, is what I did', he heard his own voice now, broken and ragged. 'Well, fuck you, mister'.

'Oh, Tone. What was wrong with *us*?'

He had never since taken a chance on happiness, though some opportunities had arisen: women who did not understand his lack of presence, who were confounded by his failure to engage. One of them even told him that sexual rejection was the one thing she, as a woman, had never had to deal with before.

In truth, Tony had never cared for anyone since Dora. Neither had he enjoyed the taste of food, the sound of rain, the warmth of a fire. He told himself he had anhedonia, and that explained everything. The impossibility of happiness; indifference as lifestyle. He had lost the ability to be moved. If Dora had ever wished revenge on him for ruining her dreams, her wish had been granted.

Was he overreacting? It was entirely possible. He was good at that. It came naturally to him. Tony now fell to unconsciousness and stars in a sudden welcome blackout: shattered at the centre of a blast of remorse, with only petals for shrapnel.

When he came to, he was still drunk. He guessed by the clock on the shelf over the toilet that it had taken his brain thirty minutes to figure out what had happened and to reboot his crazy body's messed-up operating system. He felt like a human running on Windows '95: full of glitches and prone to losing everything. Bewildered, he lay on the floor, unsure of how serious he had been or how much of his desire for death had been fuelled by alcohol and self-disgust. Whatever, as much as he did not want to go on living, he no longer felt like killing himself.

Tony opened his eyes to check if there was anything he shouldn't see. Concussion had given him a sharp headache and alcohol had dulled it, so he was in a state of numb suspension. The scalpel had made a cut along his right thigh as he slid, mocking his intentions, but he hardly felt the pain. Probably should get a tetanus shot.

He heard scratching at the door of the bathroom. Dora appeared to be standing there naked and staring at him with pity.

'Fuck off'. He understood the apparition to be merely an hallucination born of drunkenness. It was his subconscious plagiarising *An American Werewolf in London*. He had heard of people seeing ghosts of living people, but he did not believe in them himself. Then he blinked and she was gone. At least she had been naked; that was nice.

Moments later, Tony's skin felt a bit less wet and oily though his hair was still moist. The blood on his thigh had congealed and left a small matt pool on the tiled floor. His right arm and leg were bruised from the fall. His head had begun to hurt like hell.

Consciousness, fine in its place, he found unwelcome now. Gradually he eased himself up on his elbows but collapsed again. Gravity, his old nemesis, did its work. Bathwater on the floor had kept the heels of his feet wet. He drew them away from the water so as not to repeat his slip. Now he had some thinking to do and he had never done his best thinking while lying on the bathroom floor, bleeding to death.

Gingerly, Tony got up, sat on the toilet and looked down at the tainted scalpel. His head spun a little. Damage assessment: bruises earned by stupidity; nothing he would be able to brag about. Not love bites. He reached to pick the scalpel off the floor and holding it blade-down for safety, raised it above his head and put it on the shelf. Waving a hand in the bath, he felt the lukewarm current, hoping for tiny sharks, then yanked the chain and pulled the plug. The departing water built to a gurgle and left a hint of citrus in the air.

Behind the hot tap on the sink he had left his cigarettes and lighter. He got a smoke, lit up and puffed away, consoling himself that at least he would eventually succeed in killing himself. What sounded like a phrase in Klingon came to his throat then clarified into a coughing fit. 'Today is not a good day to die', he translated when it subsided.

He tried to remember what he had been thinking: some self-absorbed crap about love. He had a tendency to anti-mythologise things so that nothing was really as good as it seemed. Similarly, nothing was really as bad as it seemed, but he didn't want to know that.

As though it would protect him, Tony determined that from now on he would be untouchable. He had gone to the brink and been rejected, like a man throwing himself off the Cliffs of Moher and being hurled back to safety by a powerful, malicious gust. If this was not a signal to live, he did not know what was, but was it green or amber? He tossed the cigarette into the sink and let it hiss. He got up and examined his leg and felt nervous at having to acknowledge the pain at all but there it was in bruises left over from his cancelled crucifixion, the devil's mark of the scalpel cut. Purple clouds had broken under the skin of his leg, storming his interior landscape as thunder cleared in his head. Tony had banged it well.

Although he was still technically drunk, it was time to spring into action. He would fix the things he had done wrong. He would make peace with Dora, whether she wanted him to or not. It was years too late, but he would try.

'Stupid wanker', he said. Having tested the grunt of his own voice he did not like it one bit. It sounded weird coming from the lips of a damned drunken fool although it didn't feel strange now to be talking to himself.

There was the serious business of self-hatred to attend to, a task fit to be undertaken only during a monstrous hangover of the kind he now gloried in. If you can't hate yourself, how can you hope to hate someone else? He regarded his body in the mirror. Rising in his chest at the sight, bile and alcohol and sickness welled up in him. That was a start. Hating himself could wait. First he had to vomit. Tony Bright, reformed cynic, threw up into the sink, leaning over and heaving until he could retch no more.

Monday morning, Tony called work, saying he was really, really sick actually; and asking would they miss him terribly if he wasn't going to be in.

'What kind of sick?' the receptionist teased. 'Influenza-sick or priest-sick?'

'Sober', he groaned. 'I feel unusual. See you tomorrow. If anything urgent happens, give me a call, but I'm really, really ...'

She put him on hold and he took a moment before hanging up.

It was about ten o'clock. He had slept for thirteen hours in this stale flat contaminated with a residual sickroom stench, the rooms irradiated with vomit fallout.

He showered and scrubbed his body all over with a loofah that was caked and hard but soon softened up. He turned on the convector fan to get rid of the smell. Somebody must have disembowelled a cat in here. Someone else must have eaten the cat's innards using the inside of his skull as a plate, and forgotten to do the dishes. Then he remembered that someone had tried to kill himself and failed, crashing out on the tiles. Oh well. He hadn't been serious about it, he now knew, only full of shit. He should have looked at the scalpel, laughed like a loon and put it to one side. He should have told himself to get a grip on his own personality issues instead.

Tony took care over getting dressed. He chose a black shirt, black trousers, black socks, black shoes. He was in a black mood. It was a black day outside.

He opened the fridge. There was food in it. One banana and half a pound of butter. He brewed coffee, black, and took it in the living room while he thought about his next move, glad now that there would actually be a next move. He recalled having made some kind of ass of himself the day before but at least he had not done it in public. Dora's name hit him in each eyeball like a moment of temporary synaesthesia. Oh yes. He had to do something about Dora. Wasn't that the plan? At least there was a plan.

So he picked up the phone and called Dora at home.

There was no answer.

Tony looked up her work number in the *Golden Pages*. He had heard that she worked in a gallery now.

'You have reached the Opal Flame Arthaus. Leave your message after the raised tone'.

He felt that this lame attempt at humour gave him the moral advantage. 'Hi, this is Tony, calling for Dora'.

She picked up. 'Hi. I know you, don't I?'

'I think you do'.

He had not expected that her voice would sound weird to him, though it was definitely her voice.

'It's you', she said. 'Oh god, it's you. Why are you calling me?' Then, 'Mnnh, Conor'.

'Conor?'

'He's mounting a piece of art. Me! We've – ha! We've been smoking which is just as well because you're not someone I thought I'd ever hear from again, mister'.

'You've … changed'.

'Hold on, Conor, gotta take this'. A brief fumble with the handset. 'Ok. What do you want and why haven't you called me in the last million years?'

'I thought you didn't want me to!'

A voice in the background said, 'Do, love, who is it?'

Do. He hated that contraction, one he never even thought of making. They must have been having sex in the gallery, shutters down (or not), art upstaged.

'Sorry?' Dora said to Tony.

'I said', Tony repeated, 'I just wanted to say sorry'.

'That's what I just said. Listen, it's not a good time for me. Well, actually, it is a very good time for me, but, well, you – Ow! I have to go. Gotta go. Call me later'.

'I want you back!' What a blurt.

She had not heard him and that might be for the best. He put the phone down and slunk into the kitchen to pour his coffee down the sink and open a bottle of wine.

A minute later the phone rang again. He was standing by the sink, trembling, lighting a cigarette, having very quickly downed one full glass of something red and tannic. He let the machine take the call.

There she was, stoned Do. No longer Dora, she and her lover were making an obscene phone call to him. Either she was too high to hang up properly or had hit redial by mistake.

Intrigued and appalled, Tony poured another glass of wine and sipped as the rutting on the answering machine continued. His Dora was crying out some tosser's name, rhythmically, like an audience-of-one on the Jerry Springer show. 'Conor. Conor. Conor. Conor'.

Tony gulped down his second glass.

He could use the tape later as a particularly debasing porno experience.

To hell with it, he could use it now.

But first, another glass, which he poured and swallowed from in the kitchen before going into the living room to be nearer to the phone. Tony shifted the glass to his left hand and started to masturbate with his right, suddenly ambidextrous as Dora continued to have sex on his answering machine and her boyfriend joined in with the name-calling.

'Con. Do. Con. Do. Con. Do. Con. Do'.

Tony expected Philip Glass to walk into the room and sue the machine for royalties.

Tomorrow he would ask himself just how he could reconcile being so deeply sorry for himself and utterly shallow at the same time. Surely he was not generally that good at multitasking, despite his current talent for it. Tomorrow would do for all that personal improvement he had promised. Tomorrow he would start sorting out his life. 'Tomorrow' was a word he liked the sound of.

Meanwhile, for the first time in years, he heard Dora come like – so he told himself – Chernobyl blowing up inside Mount Etna. If he recalled correctly, she had never sounded quite as keen with him.

III

Tony poured a drink – the red wine of courage – and sat in the living room by the telephone. He drained the glass and filled it again. Courage was something you could not get all at once; you needed to apply it in layers or it would start to flake. Following that logic, he drank the second glass and poured a third, just to have it near in case extra bravery was called for. Thus fortified, he reached for the telephone and called Dora at home, expecting her not to pick up.

She picked up. Luckily, he now had courage on his side.

'Dora, it's Tony', he said.

'Tone', Dora said. 'Is that you?' Clearly she had come down at some point in the last day or so. Clearly no one was attempting to mount her just this minute.

'Yeah, me'. His voice was laced with alcohol, he now heard. Oh God. If he noticed this, he wasn't drunk enough.

'What are you doing calling me?' She sounded off-guard but most likely wasn't. Tricky things, phone conversations. No body language.

'You said to call', he slurred.

'Oh, did I?' Dora sounded relaxed. 'I don't remember that'.

'You were very stoned at the time'. Good answer.

'Right. Ok. So, Tone, what do you think I can do for you?' Listening for a moment while he said nothing, Dora must have heard his breathing. 'Have you been drinking?'

'Are you still seeing that soap actor?'

'You sound as if you've been drinking. Are you all right?'

'Maybe I am, maybe I'm not. Dora, I want to see you. I want to talk to you'.

'O … k'. Dora said. 'I'm not calling the cops just yet, so go on …'

His heart began tripping over itself. She was not the Dora he remembered. She was probably still 'Do'. He had hoped she would have changed back by now.

'Dora', he said. 'I want to start by, well, apologising'.

A moment of silence in remembrance of all his sins.

'Dora?'

'Sorry, Tone. I was just picking my jaw off the ground'.

Dora's voice. Dreamy but sarcastic. He must have blocked out in his previous reminiscences the fact that she could be sharp when required. In any case, this was not the time for sentimentality so he came straight to the point. 'Dora, I want to say how sorry I am for being an asshole when we were together'.

'Well, Tone, you should have said how sorry you were for being an asshole, *when* we were together –'

'I know. Listen'. He hoped she wouldn't hang up before he got a chance to finish.

'I'm listening'.

'I want to say sorry for what I said, all that stuff about not settling down with you. For hindering your natural progress as a woman.

'I want to say sorry for the time I suggested that if we were ever going to break up, I'd hope we could still be friends afterwards.

'Sorry for –'

'Is this going to take long?' Dora asked. 'It's just that I'm having dinner with my boyfriend on Thursday and I promised I wouldn't be late. Also, you are drunk and I don't want you saying anything you'll regret later'.

'Listen, will you? A lot of things have changed'.

'Are you all right? Is this why you called? You want to be all right?'

'Just let me confess, will you?' Tony picked up the third glass of wine and waved it insistently. 'Listen, Dora, I'm sorry for not liking your family. Especially your City wanker brother-in-law, who you didn't like either. Sorry for not seeing the bigger picture more often, or once, even. Sorry for not living up to the idea you had of the two of us happy. I mean, for not knowing what a good thing I had when I had it until I lost it'.

'Have you made a list? Tone, you've made a list. Oh, God', she said, and sounded amused. 'Aren't you going to tell me that you're just a boy standing in front of a girl asking her to fuck him?'

He welcomed her sarcasm now. He deserved it. He continued, righteous and relieved. He had some more wine. 'I'm sorry for everything, in fact'.

'Everything?'

'Yes, everything'.

'The 1958 Munich Air Disaster?'

'That wasn't me'.

A brief, crackling silence followed as he ran out of things to atone for. Thankfully, Dora helped him out.

'Are you sorry', she said, 'for the time you flirted with my sister on the dance floor in Whelan's?'

'I never! That is a horrible thing to suggest!'

'Ignorance of the law is no excuse. Are you sorry for the time when we were making love and you watched telly at the same time?'

Damn, he thought. She remembers stuff. Oh well. Sheep, lamb. 'Abso-fucking-lutely', he admitted, making a big show of this particular apology. 'It wasn't even a good episode'.

'The television wasn't even on! You just *stared* at it'.

'What?' He drank some more.

'Now', Dora said, 'for the big one. Are you sorry for the time you slept with your ex and didn't tell me?'

'I didn't tell you?'

'She did'.

'Bugger'.

'Well, never mind', Dora said. 'Bitch should have kept her mouth shut. Both times'.

'Ouch'. He realised something. 'Dora! *You* have a list! In your head!'

'Yes, dear. So, are you sorry for forgetting my birthday in 1996?'

'Did I?'

'Yes. And you forgot our anniversary, also in 1996'.

'I was having a bad year', he said, the weight of shame beginning to press down now like one small stone after another being placed on a punishment door under which he was being gradually crushed.

Dora had more stones in her hand. 'Are you sorry for the time I asked if I looked fat and you said that, all joking aside –'

'Did I say that?' Tony could not remember.

'No, I made that one up'.

'Stop fucking with me!' He drank yet more.

'And are you sorry', Dora continued, 'for the next time I asked if I looked fat and you said, "No, not really"?'

'I don't wanna play anymore', he said. 'How's the actor?'

'Unemployed, of course. The show got cancelled'.

'And you're still with him?' Tony sighed.

'Are you sorry for all the times you made me cry?'

'Made you cry? *Made you cry?* Could you be more specific? You were like a sore! You wouldn't stop weeping! That was never my fault. Well, not all the time'.

'Granted. I had my off days. Mostly Tuesdays'.

'You weren't too fond of Wednesdays either'.

'Wednesdays, schmednesdays. Are you sorry for the time we made love with all the lightning and everything?'

'Oh, you remember that. No, of course not, you … you *wench*! How could you even *suggest* that?'

'Good. Ah'.

That was important for him to hear, he felt, and he celebrated by finishing the glass of wine.

On the phone there came another crackly silence. The background sound of the universe, apparently.

'Can we have a coffee?' Tony sighed. It was now or never. Time to take their new relationship to the next level. He put the glass down on the telephone table but the table persisted in not being where his hand thought it was and the glass fell to the floor with a crump. Miraculously it didn't break but it did bleed a little.

'Can we have a coffee?' Tony repeated.

Another pause before she came back on the line. 'Oh', Dora said, all wearily now, 'if you insist'.

'Great!' he said. 'Delight in an hour!'

'Darling, I delight in every hour', she said, 'but you'd better have some coffee first, Tone, because it sounds like you've been drinking'.

A baked-bread aroma wafted in the atmosphere in Delight. Without remarking on it, Tony and Dora sat in the same booth they had sat in the last time they had come here.

She was beautiful, just as he remembered her. Cute with black hair and a large smile that she kept in reserve for special occasions, which were whenever she said they were. She had filled out a bit since he'd seen her last, but he found her more gorgeous than ever. The passage of time seemed to have given her a free ride. 'Lots of free rides', his alcoholic jealous inner child echoed back. What was happening to him? The wine had not been that strong.

Dora was wearing that fragrance, the scent he never remembered the name of but which now brought him back to several individual moments and hit his small brain with a major memory-attack, as if the VHS tape of his mind had become worn at the good bits.

They were having coffee. No food. Dora did not want to eat late at night, as it might give her nightmares and she had to be up early in the morning to help hang an exhibition. Apparently, coffee did not keep her awake.

Tony hoped that there would not be any Nick Cave on the café's stereo during their visit. So far, so good. A Queen song played now, which was fine by him.

'So', he said, after they had made small talk, 'I sobered up before coming out. It seems decadent to have more coffee'.

'You sobered up. Good. I'll give you your achievement badge later'. Dora picked up her coffee and sipped. 'I didn't expect you to call me again after yesterday'.

'What on Earth convinced you to see me?'

'You made me laugh on the phone. I let my standards slip. One of those'.

'That's not a bad thing', he said, 'letting your standards slip'.

'On the contrary'.

'My God, you've changed'.

'Everybody changes', Dora said. 'It's been an awfully long time, Tone. I mean, are you still, do you still have feelings for me? I'm kind of worried about that. God knows why'.

He drank some of his coffee. It tasted wrong. One of the waiters stood a few feet away, apparently staring at Tony with murder in his heart. Either they had not ordered enough coffee or the waiter was in love with Dora. Or Tony.

'I wanted to apologise', Tony said, a trace of wooziness in amongst his ramshackle syllables. 'No, listen, I really wanted to apologise because an awful lot of nothing has happened in the last while and it sort of made me think I just wanted to set things straight between us'.

'Really?'

'Really'.

Dora released a sad and bitter smile like the one he had last seen when she was dumping him. It was laced with the energy of unspent tears. 'You know I didn't mean to come over all smart-ass on the phone, but you sort of, you kind of put me up to it'.

'I did?'

'You started in with all that apology stuff and – I don't know, I suppose I got carried away. It's not every day a girl gets apologised to so comprehensively'.

A couple of customers shuffled in. Probably a whore with her john. Or a perfectly respectable couple. Or a whore with her john were what constituted a perfectly respectable couple these days.

'I really am sorry', he said, 'though it's obviously much too late to say it'.

'It's never too late', Dora said. She looked around to see who might be listening. Nobody she knew. 'So, what was that you said about nothing? Are you ok?'

'Not really. I miss you'.

'Then why haven't you called me before now? Surely everything can't have been going that brilliantly for you'.

'I called you yesterday. Remember?'

'Oh yeah'. She looked a little embarrassed. 'Gosh, but I'm sorry, Tone. You were never meant to hear that. We were very, very high at the time. We must have hit the redial button by mistake'.

'I kept the recording on the answering machine'.

Dora hid her smile sharply. 'Oh no. Have you been beating off to that?'

'Of course not. Jesus, Dora. What do you take me for? Well, as I said', Tony got out his cigarettes and lit up. Dora took one too, which he also lit. There they were, smoking together, like in the old days. Something in him responded to this; he felt warm towards her as she was now.

'So as I said', he continued, 'I wanted things to be straight between us'.

'Things are straight between us, sweetie', Dora said. 'We broke up'. She blew a smoke ring at him. He found it sexy as hell.

'Not like that. I mean, the Nick Cave gig. What was that all about?'

'I suppose it must have looked a little crazy to you, darling, but I was trying to provoke your interest'.

'Provoke my interest?'

'You were lethargic, a depressed mope-monster, unable to enjoy anything, and you certainly didn't seem to have any interest in me, *what*soever'.

'Really? I thought I was being an existentialist'.

'We've done sarcastic, babe'.

'We have?'

'I waited for you. I thought you'd call me and we'd make up and then we could have a conversation about it and a make-up shag. But you, you sperm-brain, you little shithead, you went away and moped'.

He sighed at the truth of it. 'I have a Ph.D. in Mopology'.

'Don't', Dora looked at him with what he took to be regret. 'Just don't'.

He wanted to die on the spot but found bravado again.

'It's OK. That's all over now', Tony assured her. 'I really was depressed though. A doctor more or less told me that once. Kind of'.

'I knew that', Dora said, 'but it didn't help me. I turned it over in my mind for ages. Then I figured you weren't going to call'.

'God, Dora, if you knew I was depressed, why didn't you say so?'

'I didn't know what to do. All I saw was this wall of nothing. You gave me nothing. I can't make something out of nothing. I'm really sorry, but I think this has to be water under the bridge. I can't help you now. You have to help yourself'.

He drank more coffee and had a notion that the coffee was beginning to take it personally. 'Dora –'

One small tear in her eye. 'You could have had a lovely life with me, Tony. We were good'.

'We were good', Tony said hopefully. 'We still could be'.

Dora recoiled as though a fly had buzzed her eyelid. 'I'm with someone'.

'The actor'. Tony heard himself sounding more upset than he meant to.

'His name is Conor'.

'How long has it been?'

'How long has it been since the Cave gig? Don't you get it, Tone? It's over. We're over. We fucked up. You fucked up'.

One of the prostitutes at another table eyed him, assessing him as a future prospect. At least someone wanted him.

Tony sighed. 'I –'

'You broke my heart', Dora continued. 'Did you know that, Tone, did you know it? I felt I'd get old just waiting for you to make up your mind'.

'Yeah but that actor. Did you give him your number right there and then?' was all he could think of to say.

'No, I did not. That shit was me flirting so you'd notice. That wasn't me asking him out. That didn't start until I'd given up on you. I waited so damn long, you have no idea. Then I figured why the hell not. Rebound fuck. I looked up his agent, pretended I wanted to cast him in a play'.

'Ingenious'.

'I thought so. He was miffed to find out it was only someone who wanted to ask him out on a date rather than give him a job. You know actors'.

Dora sat back in the plush leatherette of the booth. She regarded him for many moments, stung by the memories they were raking over.

'What about the security guy?' he asked. He wanted to remind her now. Her turn to say sorry. 'You told me you used your mouth to get those VIP passes. I was really quite upset about that, you know'.

'You were?' Dora seemed surprised.

'I was. You, using your mouth and all'.

'Oh, Jesus'. One sharp laugh. 'Of *course* I used my mouth. I *asked* him'.

Tony took a moment. 'You *asked* him?'

'Tony Supposedly Bright', Dora said. 'You never knew what you had'.

'I know it now. I just wanted to be sure', he said. 'I have some very special memories of you and me together. Really brilliant. I shouldn't have done this'.

'Charming', Dora said. 'Did you get what you needed? You were the one who hurt me, you know'.

'So', Tony said. 'Where's your man tonight?'

'He's in the pub. What do you care? He's none of your business. Tone, you're getting stupid now'.

'I hear his show might get cancelled'.

'I just told you on the phone, idiot. It's already cancelled'.

The music changed from "I'm Going Slightly Mad" to "The Invisible Man". The waiter came around to see if they needed anything. Dora smiled at him no and he butted out.

'I hate Queen', she said. 'Anyway. Aren't you going to ask me what I've been doing these past two years?'

'Yes. I was just getting around to it'.

'Precisely nothing, is what I've been doing'.

'Oh. I thought you were going to tell me you'd founded a charity and were heading off to some bird sanctuary for two years to help wash up after an oil spill'.

'I thought about working in Rwanda'.

'Rwanda? Why didn't you?'

'I hate the sight of blood that isn't my own'. Dora stubbed her cigarette out in the ashtray. 'I've actually just been working in the gallery, doing not much, really. Life makes no sense, Tone, if you don't do something'.

'It doesn't, does it?'

'No'. She shook her head. Now she seemed anxious to be away but he wanted to talk more, to hang on to whatever shred of her he could.

'Are you and the actor getting a house together any time soon?'

'He's an actor'.

'Of course. Are you staying together, though?'

'I have to go to the bathroom', Dora said. 'Can we not just be friends, Tone, even if it's friends who never see each other?'

'We could'.

'Good', she said. 'We're making progress'. Dora edged out of the booth and went to the bathroom. The potentially murderous waiter came and refilled their cups. Tony wondered what the guy might have to say on the subject of meeting your exes, but was afraid it might be derogatory, so he didn't ask.

Dora returned a few minutes later. 'Ah', she said. 'The coffee fairies have been and left something hot'. She sat down and drank some and made a face.

'Did you have a good pee?'

Dora put down her cup and looked him in the eye. 'I missed you, you know', she said. 'I missed you so fucking much'.

'Oh, Dora, if only you knew how much I missed you'.

She leaned over. He moved closer and put his hands on the table. She took them in hers and stroked them both gently. 'Listen', Dora said. 'I told you I'm with the actor. Things are going well. He proposed'.

'Does that mean ...?' Tony hoped that she was being ironic.

'It's been too long'. Dora let go of his hands.

Something finally clicked. He found himself appalled and relieved at once. 'Ok', he said. 'Apology accepted?'

'Yes'.

'Thanks', he said. 'I mean it'.

'I mean it too. Now –'

'There's just one more thing …' He knew now that this was why he had needed all that courage. This was the question of questions, the only one that mattered. Did she know what he was going to ask? 'Are you happy, Dora? I suppose I only wanted to know that you're happy'. There. He'd got it out and had not fallen over the words.

Dora was moved. There was definitely movement. 'Yes, I'm happy'.

'I'm so glad'.

'I'm glad too', she said. 'Now off you go and have a life or whatever it is you're having'.

'And if I see you in the street', he said, 'you won't blank me?'

Dora gave that bitter smile again. 'Of course not. In a while we can meet for a coffee'.

The door of intimacy was closing but he felt blessed to have been given a peek through it. 'You call me, ok?'

'No promises', she said. 'Let's go, will we?'

'Right, let's', Tony said. 'You know I'd give my left kidney to be back with you again'.

'You would?'

'But not as you are now'.

'Oh, Tone', Dora was almost tender, '*Nul points*'.

Tony insisted on paying. He and Dora walked out of Delight together. Another pair of what he took to be lost souls, pushed past them to enter.

'Rude!' Tony said and Dora tapped him on the arm to shush him.

They stood a moment looking at each other. He took in her face so that he could remember it as it was now, just in case he never saw her again. That face was a little fuller with a few more crows' feet than the last time. 'You're really something', he said. 'Dora, you're beautiful'.

'Thanks'. Dora tossed a glance to her left. 'I'm going this way'.

'I'm going the other way'.

'You see?'

A line of cars gathered slowly at the lights.

'Right, so'.

'Just one more thing', Dora said. 'One more "one more thing". If we do meet for a coffee, let's not go to this place again'.

'Yes, Columbo', Tony said and gazed at her and wondered what to do now. 'You've changed, Dora'.

'That I have', she said.

'What happened?'

'You, Tone'. Dora frowned. 'You happened'.

'Yeah', he said. 'I did'.

Dora Potts touched his elbow gently then withdrew and turned away. Tony stood alone. He watched her walk into the dark until she was finally gone, until she had melted into the night like she was nobody in particular.

The Negative Cutter

Episode I

Thunder fucked the sky. A sonic boom broke in the air and died away. The bedroom window rattled, distorting the face of a waxing gibbous moon that flung droplet shadows at the opposite wall. Krista was unperturbed by the sudden blast of noise. She and Raimi had not been sleeping. Now she turned over into the empty warm depression that still held his fading aftershave, a scent known as *Fadó*. There was another odour too, of mint and latex and the byproducts of degrading cells. Without much thought she picked the condom up from the sheet and flung it at the basket beside the TV; for the first time that night, her lover's seed found a target. She listened to his urine sloshing into the bowl before the change of note as he ran the tap to wash his hands and the pipes set up a screech that would not die for minutes yet. Krista hated how Raimi wasted water like he had invented it.

On the TV news, a Shoga reported a bombing at Vincent's Children's Unit. The C-Specials suspected the Anglican Militia but Krista knew that the Legion had been responsible.

Raimi returned to the futon and wrapped her in his arms.

'That was nice', she said.

'Did you come?'

'Yeah', Krista whispered. 'Three times'.

Her lover grinned like an Olympic Village idiot expecting a bronze.

'Once in the shower this morning', Krista said, 'and twice in the cellar, at work'.

Raimi recalled the day's events. A junior offline editor at Purgatory Ltd, he was working on a remake of *All The President's Men*. This new take on the material was a Curtisian comedy that concerned the four concurrent love affairs of a fictional Irish Head of State. She conducted these trysts while being investigated by a pair of hard-bitten lifestyle reporters for alleged crimes against fashion; and while her estranged father lay dying in the Blackrock Clinic. It was a period piece.

Shortly after noon, two C-Specials had arrived to seize the files. Barging past reception they demanded to see the boss, Elaine Brooks, who stormed out of her office and told the cops where to go. This film was an important piece of romantic-comedy entertainment, and the police had no right to stop it. Besides, you couldn't seize a file. There were backups at six locations around the world. The film would continue to be made, even if it wasn't made here. You can't stop the signal, she told them. The only effect of this seizure would be to take work out of the economy.

Nonetheless the Specials Commander showed her the warrant. That changed the situation. Having no choice, Brooks gave in. A sanction at the Tribunal would shut her down. Emboldened, the Commander declared this production to be flagrantly in contravention of the blasphemy law. She demanded that the files be purged. Then she delivered an injunction forbidding Purgatory Ltd to do any further work on this film. Raimi expected that lunch would be cancelled too.

From the door of his office he watched the goings on with shock and impotence, wrapped in dread. All the while Brooks did not look once in his direction. Something told him that was not good.

He suspected that the real reason the film was being shut down was fear. The protagonist was Muslim and female and uncircumcised and the President of Ireland. The film had the potential to give great offence to believers. The Commander seemed to read his mind. She said that apart from anything else this was a matter of public safety. A film like that at the Savoy –

The files would have to be destroyed. Not just deleted, destroyed. Brooks asked what that involved, exactly. What extra steps must she take?

Raimi, still looking out, wondered why the Specials hadn't just executed the screenwriter in the first place; which executive had greenlit such a film to be shot here; and whether anyone had paid attention to the market conditions.

Finally reacting, he retreated into Edit One and locked the door. He wouldn't be party to this, although Brooks did not need to go through him to have the files expunged.

He heard the shrieking of weapons. One of the Specials was shooting a SteenbeckDigi89 in a symbolic gesture that had no practical purpose.

Eventually, as Raimi's funk subsided, he heard boots outside. It was the Specials clomping out like Cybusmen.

Raimi emerged ready for an argument and was relieved to see that the others on the floor, suddenly busy, had vanished into their offices too. None had yet come out. Brooks rounded on him and accused him of cowardice. Why didn't he have her back? Why the hell had he sodded off? Pure useless. She fumed that the SD89 was toast and would cost a fortune to replace.

He didn't dare tell her that she had a cheek lecturing him on the subject of cowardice but it wouldn't have mattered if he had. Brooks had already decided to resign from *All The President's Men* and would explain her reasons in person to the producer. This was better than facing the freakshow in the Castle.

Reluctantly, despite the inevitable commercial fallout, Raimi had to agree, although the salary cuts he expected, needed to pay for the broken equipment, would hurt.

Krista ran The Matt Talbot, a chic bar on Curved Street. That morning a mail had come through to her personal account from her husband Amiel, asking after her. The more she thought of him, the less she thought of him, although she liked his concern.

Two years before, tired of racist abuse from the native scum, Amiel had decided to leave the country and begged her to come with him to London, where he could get a job without being spat on. He took her refusal to mean that she did not love him. She had told him that she could not leave her mother, and family always came first. What was he, Amiel had asked, if not family?

Poor Amiel. He hadn't even known about Raimi. That little revelation would come later. When it did Amiel turned out to be supportive rather than upset. They were free agents now, were they not? This response made Krista feel just a little unloved. Amiel was French.

After a year, relations had warmed sufficiently that they now sent the occasional mail. Krista came to feel that although they had not been good at marriage – not that marriage – their new equilibrium seemed right. The break-up had been partly her fault, Krista knew, her own mistake. Her overestimation of Amiel's potential as a human being was the stupid miscalculation that had led her to marry him in the first place. It all settled down eventually. After her initial disappointment that he had chosen to go, even when she wouldn't join him, she found herself relieved to see the back of him. Her life was less complicated now without all the skulking around that an affair entailed.

That subterfuge had begun two months after her honeymoon, when Krista had met Raimi in a nightclub where she was the hostess. Raimi and his friends were on a work outing. He was young and thin, which she liked, and his cropped black hair and kind face were her idea of classically male; his features were soft, reminding her of the Cat in the Hat. He had the appealing aura of a certain type of man, one who, almost as a reflex, puts the needs of others before his own. For his part, Raimi had said he found her Modigliani body fiercely attractive; that kind of construction always did it for him.

Now they were both asleep and the past dreamed in their heads. There was no more thunder that night.

The alarm woke them. In the street someone was breaking into a car. The siren of the car's defence system sounded like a piece of sonic sculpture. Their sudden ejection from sleep was just as well; Krista had to be up. She raised herself from the futon, looked around and closed the window that was letting the sound in. She glanced back at Raimi. Going by the gibberish he was mouthing he was still waking from some interrupted nightmare, some other life about which she knew nothing. Krista wandered naked down the corridor to the bathroom to have her shower.

Raimi opened his eyes. He felt a hard dryness in his mouth and tried to generate saliva but only a little came out. He heard the shower running. No singing, though. No moaning either. That was odd. He had half a mind to join her but laziness got the better of desire so he pretended to be asleep until after she had dressed, eaten breakfast and left for the bar. All the time he listened to her coming and going as well as to the siren. Either someone had been carjacked or there was a German band playing outside.

He heard the front door closing and opened his eyes in response. Krista hadn't kissed him goodbye. He had fallen asleep for a few minutes after all. The siren stopped.

While he was brushing his teeth, the phone rang. He put the brush down, swallowed the toothpaste and answered the call on the bathroom's monitor. It was Elaine Brooks. She wanted him down at Purgatory pronto for a meeting with Barry LeCobbe, a producer of *All the President's Men*. Somehow she had to explain to him why Purgatory was pulling out of its contract with Fox. Brooks needed bodies in the room.

Wearily he dressed, and noted that he had been naked in front of his boss. It was already one of those days.

Krista came home from the day shift, looking exhausted. Raimi was perched in front of the TV, watching a video by The Come Along Ponds. He turned it off when Krista entered the living room.

'Hello, love'. Raimi sensed trouble. 'How was it?'

'There was a raid'. Krista closed the door behind her and sat down at the table. 'They said we were serving illegals. We weren't. I'd know. We had a Ugandan couple and a Pole and a strange little woman from Aberystwyth. Nothing to write home about and I'm sure their papers were in order. The cops cleared the place out all the same'.

'Assholes'. Raimi got up from the TV and went over to give her a shoulder rub that she did not resist. 'But let me tell you about the day I had. Fucking producers'.

Krista didn't answer. She let his fingers work on her knotted muscles. 'Can we go out tonight? I feel like getting trashed'.

Twenty minutes later they nursed a pair of pints at a small table in O'Rourke's. Krista didn't, after all, seem to have the energy for a bender.

'LeCobbe's lawyer says the master info is with Fox so that's covered but we're a liability now', Raimi said. 'He says he understands the political thing but it's not his problem and he's not going to carry it. They're taking the job away and blaming us'.

'That's bad', Krista said.

'I think the locals will know what we had to face but internationally Purgatory is screwed. Someone should have checked the paperwork or the law or we should have known it ourselves. I don't know who's to blame – could be a lot of people'.

'She's not blaming you, is she?'

'Brooks said it was out of our control. But she also said she can either let us all go and shut up shop or pitch for a government contract that's coming up. No one will give us a film now, not a proper one, and I can't say I'd blame them. Me, I vote for the government pitch'.

'You'd better. I don't want to have to go to Sylvia for the rent'.

The barman flashed the lights. Krista grimaced and drained her glass.

'Fucking curfew', Raimi said.

Holding hands, they walked down Bath Place and turned on to the seafront.

'I love Paris in the springtime', Krista said.

'It's beautiful', Raimi said.

'Paris?'

'The moon. Look at the moon'. It was ice-white in the sky, flakes of snow flickering across its face like escaped stars. On any other night he might have thought it ugly, a ghost designed by a robot. Tonight the sky was a deeper green than usual, accentuating the brightness of the lunar disc.

Later the same moonlight seeped in through the window as they lay on the futon, watching *Don't Look Now* on TV.

'This film has the most beautiful love scene in cinema history', Raimi said. 'I'm surprised it's not on the Index'.

He sighed and buried himself in Krista's hug. Her chin rested on the crown of his head. She moved her hand down and ran it gently along his thigh then brought it up between his legs. Raimi was warmed by her touch.

Some time later, long after the film had ended and the TV had turned itself off, Raimi found himself still awake. Krista was talking in her sleep about bastard policemen.

The cold morning sunlight hurt her eyes but Krista, wrapped in her blue dressing gown at the kitchen table, did not close them. She read the *Times* on a tablet while Raimi made coffee and prepared the breakfast she'd asked for, Eggs Benedict. It was his signature dish.

'Do you want to come to the movies today?' Raimi brought the breakfast plates over and sat down. '*Episode III* is on'.

'Busy'. Krista put down her tablet. 'I'm going in today'.

'Krista, are you annoyed with me or something?'

'Why would I be annoyed with you?'

'You're annoyed with me'.

'Now I am'.

Her mood didn't last. After breakfast, Raimi began to wash up. Krista teased him by dropping her gown to the kitchen floor and walking naked down the corridor. She came back carrying her clothes and put them on slowly while he watched, his hands stopped in the suds. Then she came over and slipped her arms around him from behind. 'You'll be all right without me today'.

He turned around inside her arms, holding his sudsy hands out. 'Will you be ok without me?'

She kissed him on the mouth, a quick lip-intriguing peck.

'When can I expect you back?' he asked.

'What time is your film?'

'Three'.

'You made a plan'. Krista released him. 'Well done, you'.

Although it was designed to glide silently, the Airtram scraped on the rail. It sounded like an angle-grinder and everyone was used to the buzz. Raimi sat uncomplaining like the rest. Someone would fix it one of these days. The young woman sitting opposite did not look directly at him but checked out his reflection in the window. He met her image's eye. She had the appearance of a student: well dressed, a serious expression on her face, a conservative haircut. Raimi was not sure if he could read anything from that.

At Sydney Parade an elderly woman stepped in and stood by the door. Dressed in black from head to toe, she had an old iPod clipped to her belt. No one paid much attention as she turned it on. Loud for such a little box, it played a hymn. The woman brought a crucifix from inside her big black coat, like she was going for a gun. Instead of an effigy of Jesus it bore an object that immediately made

Raimi want to throw up. It was an aborted foetus preserved in lucite, its arms missing. The thing was pinned to the cross to form an image of the Thalidomide Christ. This woman was one of the PCP nut-jobs, Raimi now recognised. Other passengers muttered amongst themselves but whether in approval or disgust he did not hear.

'Shit', Raimi said.

The young woman snorted.

The old lady called out, 'T.C. dies for your sins!'

Enough.

'Do you hear that?' Raimi demanded of the air. 'Did you hear what she just said? It's fucking appalling'.

'Who are you, to be swearing like that?' the serious young woman asked. 'You N-word. That's what you are'.

Raimi felt like someone had slapped him about the face with a prayer leaflet. He could not find the words to reply and feared that if he did they would not be understood.

The Airtram stopped at Sandymount. Raimi got up to leave although it wasn't his stop. He had to get by the old lady and feared catching her blank eyes.

'Are you saved by Thalidomide Christ?' she asked as he passed.

Shaking his head he stepped out of the carriage.

The Airtram pulled away.

The snow had resumed. He felt the cold in his bones as he waited.

For Raimi, the best part of watching a *Star Wars* movie was the thrill he still got from the opening title sequence. He loved the martial music, the introductory crawl of expository text and the first pan, usually down, through a field of stars. After that it got complicated.

Another tram arrived. Wanting to be sure there were no crazy people among them before he chose his door, he checked out the other passengers as they boarded. They all looked normal.

There were no further incidents on the way into town but as Raimi crossed Westmoreland Street, he observed a heavy C-Specials presence. They had already placed metal barriers along the kerb on both sides.

At the IFI, only one film was showing, on all three screens: *Masturbation is a Sin*. *Revenge of the Sith* had been cancelled. Raimi had an impulse to see the Public Information Film but resisted it.

As for *Star Wars*, he lingered in the café with a latte and considered how he felt about the series. Every time he saw *Revenge of the Sith*, he found himself questioning the wisdom of asking tiny children to identify with Anakin Skywalker, this vicious slaughterer of younglings, this would-be executioner of his own offspring, this planet-killer, whose innumerable crimes tended to go unmentioned on the lunchboxes and the duvets. The children of the day had seemed to enjoy dressing up as that genocidal demon, that Hitler of Coruscant, who was so easily forgiven in the sixth episode for all his murder and depravity and cruelty, that he might have been a Catholic dictator. Not even that. Vader had made no final act of contrition, no deathbed confession, and was forgiven anyway. The little maniacs were bloodthirsty though; kids enjoyed someone else's ordeal of gore and pain and horror, each having emerged from one in the first place.

The problem with the *Star Wars* series, Raimi saw, was its facility with a lie, the supposedly moral characters' flexible ethics. This was a failing that deflated the stories for him, now that he considered the problem. Nothing much was at stake for the ordinary person in the galaxy, if each side of the Force was as mendacious as the other. This was a self-regulated, closed system. Sith and Jedi needed each other, these demigods interlocked in a duet of power, indifferent to the mortals whose lives they destroyed in the restoration or destruction of balance. Other people's lives seemed to come naturally to these superhumans.

Did not the Republic sanction slavery, and the Jedi approve it? Was not truth a function of expediency? Were not the clones considered lesser creatures than the humans? Take your superiority complex and shove it down an endless shaft, Raimi thought. In this galaxy, clones and droids and people alike were born to suffer. That was the basic fact of life, as Threepio had recognised. There was little freedom for the regular Jawa, no matter which faction of the divine duality was in charge at any one time.

This moral and ethical fickleness made no dramatic sense to Raimi but he felt drawn to the movies. There was something religious about them, something Roman.

Then he saw the point, the true meaning of *Star Wars*. It was indeed that there was something Roman about them, something religious. To any political or spiritual system, what mattered was the system. Raimi felt slightly better to have figured that one out. Tattooine looked much the same under Palpatine as under Valorum.

Deciding that he really couldn't sit through the anti-wanking film even if it contained images of women masturbating as well as men, though he suspected it had neither, just some priests giving out about females, he finished his coffee, got up and left the cinema.

On Eustace Street he began to feel nervous as a new thought came to him. What if Krista's bar was raided again today? The Matt Talbot was around the corner so he took the turn into Curved Street.

Inside, it didn't look much different from the last time he'd been. Damo was serving a customer.

'I heard what happened', Raimi said.

'Hiya', Damo was busy. 'You shouldn't come here'.

'Damo', Raimi sank into himself and didn't know where to look.

The barman shrugged then turned again to his customer. There didn't seem to be any Poles in today, or Ugandans, or strange little women from Aberystwyth.

Back on Fleet Street Raimi stopped to watch the march passing through Westmoreland. An enormous body of people swarmed like the funeral procession for a dead rock star but these were not mourners, though they chanted hymns. Banners sailed by on this swollen river of the faithful. He kept well back in case one of them had a notion to throw something at him. Other onlookers waited for a gap in the crowd and darted through. Raimi recalled a time when the Irish could march in protest all they liked and the government would ignore them. Now the government never ignored the marches, because the marches were always in support of the Progressive Christian Party, which in effect was the government, despite the hopes for influence of its junior partner, Fianna Fáil.

Raimi needed to get back to the Airtram but did not want to risk losing himself in the march. Instead he stood and took in this flood of the devout: old women wheeling prams that contained large plastic models of broken foetuses; young men bearing ecstatic expressions on their faces; women smiling blindly, botoxed by sanctity. An enormous green banner declaring *Ireland for Jesus* drifted past. Raimi snorted. Look at all these yokels, he thought. He bet that those of them who could read and write were even now mentally going over their acceptance speeches for their Darwin Awards.

Then something broke. A jolt of thunder cracked in Raimi's head for a millisecond, knocking him further back into Fleet Street. It felt to him like lightning from God.

In reflex he clasped his hands to his ears and tried to squeeze out the shock which had now resolved into a needle, a sine wave of surgical steel that was gone as soon as it had struck, leaving a hollow echo in his head, a *bip* that repeated and died. *Bip.*

The suddenness disturbed him. Had he been Tased remotely?

No. This had been over swiftly, with no palpitations.

He'd heard that noise before but could not identify it. This time it was compressed, more memory than event. No one else in the street appeared to have noticed.

His eyes were wet and he hadn't been crying.

Raimi sat down in the street to recover. It was a panic attack, some kind of switch thrown in his mind by the overwhelming power of the crowd still deluging in the street.

He knew there was no reason to tell Krista about what had happened, no point in troubling her. This was a glitch. This was just himself, finally getting old. It was only a headache that had no time to hang around; or a burst of tinnitus that had tried his brain on for size and rejected it.

Episode II

An aborted foetus floated on the main display in Edit One. In grainy black and white, the image was designed to look like an ultrascan. Time ran on at the bottom of the screen in bright red letters. Raimi did not feel that he could protest. Work was work and the government contract had saved their jobs.

Purgatory's new Supervising Editor, Reg Bellingham, sat behind him. This Yorkshireman, a veteran of the film business in England, had such stories of directors going mad on set, actors taking over the cutting, and the obscene images he'd splice into the most heartwarming films – a balanitic cock placed into a Nancy Meyers film was his favourite – that Raimi had taken to him after only a week.

Elaine had hired Bellingham to raise their game. His task for now, she had told everyone, was to sit in on edits, to see if Purgatory's crew could learn from his old-school knowledge. He was also to watch out for anything that might get them into trouble, so that they could avoid a repeat of the LeCobbe incident.

Bellingham did not seem to object to the content of their new Public Information Film. 'It's about time something meaningful came out of this place', he said.

'Meaningful my arse'. Raimi tried to sound English.

Bellingham merely smiled. 'Did you ever see one of them up close? I did. Like something Screaming Mad George would come up with'.

'One of what?' Raimi swivelled around in his chair.

'Never mind. Fellow I knew, Spall was his name', Bellingham said. 'Sparks, back in the old days. His wife was expecting so he went along to her scan and the nurse gave them a print to take home, their first family snapshot if you like. Spall had a T-shirt made up of it. He went around wearing it like he had a womb with a view'.

'Bless', Raimi said.

'It was all hunky dory at first'.

Now the foetus on the screen morphed into Dali's *Christ of Saint John of the Cross,* but suspended over a lush field. In a minute Raimi would remove the arms of the man on the cross, to transform the image into the Thalidomide Christ.

'How did the baby turn out?' Raimi asked.

'She aborted it without consulting him. So what did this Spall do? He took a rifle to a school in Redcar, shot ten kids'.

'Christ'.

'Don't know what happened to the wife'.

Raimi felt a chill. 'I haven't seen a foetus and I don't care to'.

Bellingham put his hand on Raimi's elbow. 'Is everything all right at home?'

'What do you mean?'

The older man sighed and got up to go. 'Nothing. Doughnuts?'

'Can you get us one with vanilla?'

'Right. Anything else?' Bellingham turned in the doorway.

'I could murder a coffee'.

Raimi resumed his work, bringing Dali's *Christ* back up. This job was nearly over, thank God. With a few strokes on his pad, he dissolved the arms and moved the nails so that the man on the cross was attached through his stumps.

After Bellingham returned with the doughnuts they reviewed the edited footage. When it was over, the Supervising Editor looked thoughtful.

'Do you think we've a cut we can present?' Raimi asked.

'I'd say yeah'.

Raimi closed the window and relaxed. 'Nothing to do now but wait', he said. He pressed the speaker button on his desk. 'Could we get a couple of coffees to Edit One?'

He looked at his colleague reflected in the screen and felt sad. Bellingham seemed older than his years. Raimi turned around. 'Ever had a midlife crisis?'

Bellingham frowned. 'In my thirties I ran off with an actor. You work in the business, it's inevitable, isn't it?'

'But you got back with your wife', Raimi said. Bellingham had related this story only days before but Raimi wanted something to talk about that wasn't foetal. An old man's tale of his younger self's adventures – that was the opposite of foetal.

'I learned my lesson'. Bellingham sounded happy to have done so.

'I suppose we all do, in the end'.

'When I look back on it now I don't like some of the places I've been. It gets lonely, of course, but I nearly ballsed my marriage up, didn't I?'

'I suppose we all do, in the end', Raimi repeated.

'Maura never forgave me'. Bellingham chuckled.

'Yeah. I think I'm having my mid-life crisis about ten years early'.

The coffee arrived. A new intern came in with a tray and set it down.

'That was quick', Raimi said to the young woman. She nodded at Bellingham, who was obviously impatient to continue talking. Raimi watched her go.

'I mean', Bellingham said, 'if there's one thing I learned it's this. You need someone to anchor you. You can't go on and do this thing called life all on your own. You need a higher power. A happy wife for a happy life, isn't that what they say?'

'I dunno, never heard that one before. Yeah but surely you don't regret you once had a wild side'.

'By no means. It helped in the end. It taught me what matters, that. When I reached bottom I knew who I was meant to be with'. Bellingham sounded grave. 'The cut looks good'.

Raimi switched over to the TV then picked up his coffee and sipped.

The news was on. They watched idly while waiting. The Shoga was a new model. Everyone is new this week, Raimi thought.

'The Minister for Information and Justice has denied allegations that members of his party were involved in soliciting sexual favours from boys as young as twelve ...'

Raimi switched channels. 'Fucking hell'.

Another Shoga. 'Funding has been withdrawn by Endemol following declining ratings for the Mars program. Colonist representative Sorcha Brown insists the company must now seek a new production partner to safeguard the lives of the community. Meanwhile, NASA has cancelled its proposed mission to the Kuiper Belt owing to a –'

Krista didn't seem to have heard him come in and did not acknowledge his arrival. She was in the bedroom, packing.

'Krista', Raimi stepped into the room. 'What are you doing?'

She grabbed more clothes out of the wardrobe, hangers and all. Her suitcase was too full to close properly so she threw the clothes on it and stood there looking lost. Raimi touched her shoulder but she wouldn't face him. 'Go away'.

'Krista!' He withdrew his hand and stepped back.

Krista turned. 'Forget it, Raimi. You're doing a *propaganda film* for those bastards'.

'I'll give up my job. Right now'.

'I don't care what you do'.

Raimi guided her into the kitchen and sat her down at the table. She was having some kind of fit. It would pass.

'Let's talk', he said. The softness in his voice appeared to placate her. He sat down too but did not try to hold her. He looked at her as kindly as he could. 'I don't want you to leave me'.

'You can't do that film'. Krista sniffed. 'That bloody film you told me about. You shouldn't have told me about it'.

'You said we needed to pay the rent', Raimi said. 'It was your idea that I keep on at Purgatory'.

'They beat up Damo', Krista glared at him. 'I walked out'.

'Oh now I *have* to keep my job. You can't have it both ways'. He put his hand on her arm a second time and she did not shake it away.

Krista started to cry. 'The Specials did a number on him. He's not even foreign'.

'Jesus'. Raimi sighed. 'Neither am I'.

'Then let's do something', Krista said. 'Something to show them we don't give a damn. I want to spit in those bastards' faces'.

'Ok', Raimi heard himself sounding meek; he assumed deliberately. 'What do you have in mind?'

Episode III

The iodine stink of the sea drifted in on the wind, filtered through the wire mesh that separated Blackrock Park from the Airtram line. It reminded Raimi of lost opportunities for walking on the beach of a Sunday, listening to the seagulls and the foghorn, watching the ferries and the cruise liners, smiling at dogs running to catch thrown, sea-softened wood.

Sunday was a family day out for the couples here with their kids, lying in the grass on blankets with picnics, or throwing footballs under the oaks. Today the grass seemed to have taken on an unnatural shade of green. Over by the pond, a mother pulled her toddler away from the edge. A teenage girl flew a kite, her father and mother off walking among the trees. Two C-Specials patrolled with an easygoing air. In the sky, a drone glinted at the head of a vapour trail.

After a stroll to the hillock and back, Raimi and Krista parked themselves on the concrete pier in the middle of the pond.

'We could always go ahead and form the club now', Raimi said. He watched a seagull swoop down and back up empty-beaked. 'Your small act of rebellion. Fuck 'em if they can't take a joke'.

'It was just a stupid idea', Krista said. 'I wish I hadn't thought of it'.

'It's a brilliant idea'.

A boy threw a ball into the air. One of the passing C-Specials turned and waved his gun at the boy who started to cry until his mother took him into her arms and told him not to. She glanced up at the cop, who smiled at her.

'I don't know', Krista said. 'Should we forget the whole thing and just leave while we can?'

'You're right', Raimi said.

'I can get Damo to run the club once it goes public but I can't wash our hands if they all of a sudden deny that we ever had a licence'.

'Are you prepared to go to jail?'

'I dunno'.

'Ok', he said. 'Let's do it but just among a few friends. Get a feel for it. See if you're sure'.

'We should get out', Krista said. 'But we can't leave my mother'.

'Why don't you talk to her?'

Krista appeared to consider this then she stood up. Raimi followed as she began to wander back along the pier. He held back, turning her proposition over in his mind. It was a good idea. It might get them into trouble.

Raimi noticed some children playing tag in the gazebo while their parents watched silently. Overhead, the drone had started to circle again. On the way out, he almost stepped in some dogshit. It was that kind of park.

It seemed to Raimi that O'Brien's these days lacked a certain *je ne sais pourquoi*. Years before on this site there had been an old pub with the same name. He would have liked to have been around back then, to hang out with the advertising creatives who swarmed the place on Fridays while the media crowd drank next door in the Leeson Lounge, now long shuttered. Those old days, Raimi knew, were never coming back.

Sylvia took up her glass and sipped. Hard-of-hearing, she shouted everything.

'I heard from Amiel the other day', Sylvia called out. She glanced at Raimi to gauge his reaction to the news. 'He sent me a postcard, of all things. He's taken a job at the BFI, just like Mulder and Scully'.

'That's enough about Amiel, mother'. Krista put a finger in her pint and stirred gently. She didn't raise her voice when talking to her mother.

'Hmph', Sylvia said. 'He was right, you know. You should leave this bloody country'.

A drinker at a table nearby huffed.

'Keep your voice down', Krista said.

'Even when I was your age they were there. Youth Defence, SPUC, all the cunts – but there were still too many of us with our placards'.

Raimi leant over so that Sylvia could hear. 'Ladies who march'.

She looked fondly at him.

'We were thinking of going somewhere', Krista said. 'But we also had a crazy idea'.

'Well, you'd better make it quick one', Sylvia said.

'Will you come with us?' Raimi asked.

'I'd miss my bridge. Plus', Sylvia said, 'I have news for you two'.

Krista put down her pint. 'News?'

'I've been feeling a bit unwell this past while and saw old man Stewart yesterday. Turns out I have lung cancer'.

'You're kidding'. Raimi said.

'Shit'. Krista went white. 'Why didn't you say this earlier?'

'I wanted to hear what you young ones were up to'.

Two boys and two girls walked in. They wore uniforms that neither Raimi nor Krista had seen before: all black, with épaulettes and neckerchiefs and woggles and berets. One of the kids carried a collection box marked *Youth Defence Youth Chapter*. The stupidity of that killed Raimi's mind for a second.

'Cancer'. Krista whispered. 'Lung fucking cancer'.

'Collecting for Youth!' The children passed tins among the customers in the bar. Most of the patrons handed over coins without complaint.

When one of the girls arrived at their table, Krista wanted to tell her to piss off, but Sylvia seemed happy to talk to this young lady.

'Collecting for Youth'. The girl shoved her tin at Sylvia.

'What's your name, dear?'

Krista scowled. 'We're trying to talk'.

The girl ignored her. 'Sister Michael is my name'.

'But what name did your mother give you?'

'Collecting for Youth. Now are you going to hand over the cash, you old biddy?'

Raimi glanced concern at Krista.

'Do you have a mother?' Sylvia asked. Even shouting, she sounded kind.

'She died giving birth to me'. The uniformed child had an empty face.

'Here'. Krista took a coin out of her pocket and pushed it into the slot in the lid of the tin. 'Now get the fuck out of here'.

'Blasphemy', the girl hissed.

'What she said', Raimi addressed the girl. 'Get the fuck out of here'.

Quickly she pulled a phone out of her pocket and snapped a photograph of Raimi. 'N-word'. She skipped off to join her colleagues gathered at the other end of the bar before leaving.

'She took my picture!'

'They can't do anything to you', Krista said.

'When I was her age ...' Sylvia began, but her voice trailed off. She appeared to be staring at a distant ghost, perhaps her own.

'Time now, ladies and gents! Curfew!' the barman called, though it was only nine-thirty.

Raimi felt a cold twinge in his chest.

'Mum, let's go', Krista said. 'We need to talk'.

'Yes, let's'.

They left the pub without finishing their drinks.

Dodging a speeding car on the way, Raimi and Krista walked Sylvia across the road to the gates of New Mespil.

'It's going to take us half an hour to get home', Raimi said.

'Then you go and I'll spend the night with mum. We have to talk'. Krista hugged him and kissed him goodnight.

Krista and Sylvia went in.

Cancer. The word hung hollow in Raimi's head. He walked to the taxi rank outside the Burlo. There were three cabs and nobody waiting. He got in the first one. The safety Shoga said, 'Belt up, right?' Then it laughed half-heartedly. Who the hell, Raimi fumed silently, did it think it was?

'Where to, bud?' the driver asked.

'Blackrock, please. Into the village'.

The driver moved out and headed south. He turned on the TV in the seat-rest. Another Shoga came on, this one in mid-report 'In response to the government's suspension of cross-border bodies, the Anglican Militia Army Council today announced a resumption of its armed struggle. There have been no incidents reported so far …'

'That's going to be fun', Raimi said.

The Shoga continued '… spokesman said the Militia could not stand by and watch the severing of democratically mandated legislative links with the Six Counties. He warned the terrorists that any action by the Anglicans will force the administration to retaliate. In other news the Taoiseach today condemned last week's rally by the Republican activist group Saoirse in Cork. He assures the public that his government is fully committed to …'

'What's with the sudden curfew?' Raimi asked.

'They can have a curfew all they want', the driver said, 'but I'm out until four, and that's that'.

'A man who's happy in his work'.

'I don't think they've put up roadblocks yet', the driver said. 'What do you do yourself?'

'Nothing'.

'I'd say there's great money in that'.

In the back seat, Raimi folded his arms around his shoulders and pretended that he was in an airplane about to crash. As the car sped past RTÉ, he looked out and saw that the buildings were surrounded by C-Specials' APCs, their lights flashing. A drone twinkled in the sky above them.

At home Raimi turned to Channel 63 to find a movie but the signal was scrambled so he switched to 154. The Shoga said, '… in an incident in Sligo, Ireland, this evening, the Silver Swan Hotel was devastated by a lorry bomb. And it was *not* a keg of Guinness exploding. So far, nobody has claimed responsibility, but sources indic-c-c-cate it could be the work of the Anglican Militia who announced the resumption of their campaign earlier in the day. Yes folks, they're *back*. And now, some p-p-p-oetry'.

They're back. It dawned on Raimi that there had not been an Anglican Militia before the election so how could they be back? The only terrorist activity he had known about was that carried out by the Legion.

He turned the sound off then went into the kitchen to find the joint he had rolled earlier with the last of the dope Damo had given to Krista. He lit up and before settling into an armchair to smoke, opened the window, letting the sound of the sea wash into the room. He reached out, found the remote on the floor and pushed the button for music. Pink Floyd's *Wish You Were Here* album snaked its mellow scales through the speakers. Poor Sylvia, he thought. Cancer. That's going to wreck her buzz.

Outside, the foghorn eructated. Raimi heard sirens in the street but felt sure they were not coming for him. He took a long toke from the joint, the smoke catching in his lungs as he held his breath. Soon he could hold it no longer and he coughed.

David Gilmour sang. Raimi listened for several minutes then the music went dead. Something had happened to the connection, just as he was getting into his high.

'Damn', Raimi said, his voice appearing to stretch out before him as though the sound had taken physical form. 'There's always something'.

Krista settled on the couch in her mother's living room, which was small and decorated minimally, reflecting Sylvia's simple tastes. She had no TV, but her bookshelves were stuffed with hardbacks. Sylvia was a great reader, a trait she had tried to pass on to her daughter but without success. While she waited for the tea, Krista looked over one of the shelves. It hadn't occurred to her before to check out her mother's library. Going by its contents, she saw that Sylvia liked the books of Joyce Carol Oates, who, it appeared, had written quite a few.

'Here you are, dear'. Sylvia emerged from the kitchen with a tea tray, which she set on the low table in front of the couch then sat down.

'Thanks, mum'.

'I'm glad you're staying over'. Sylvia poured the tea.

'I'm a little bloody shaken at your news', Krista said. She wished her mother could speak softly.

'I suppose. It isn't every day you get told you've only six months'.

Krista shook her head. 'There's nothing to be done?'

'They don't have that kind of therapy here'. Sylvia set a cup of tea before Krista then sat down. 'Believe me, I've looked into it. I even went to a witchdoctor last week. Turned out to be a Catholic witchdoctor'.

'I don't really know what to say'. Krista's cup trembled in her hand.

'We all have to go some time. And before I do, I have a little nest egg put away. I want you to have it. Use it to get out'.

Krista sipped her tea. 'I'm going to stay and look after you, mum'.

Sylvia didn't seem to hear. 'You never talk about Raimi. Does he have a dad?'

'His father died when he was twelve. His mother moved to Australia when he was eighteen. He doesn't talk about them'.

'I'm glad you have him. I was always in two minds about that Amiel'.

Krista put down her cup. 'Mum, why did he send you a postcard? He emails me but I didn't know you were in touch with him'.

'Oh dear'.

'What do you mean?'

'Daughter, your old husband still wants to save you, the poor thing. The postcard was to persuade me to convince you'.

'I don't need his help'. Krista had an image in her mind of a distraught Raimi waving goodbye to her at the port. The man-child looked lost without her. She couldn't do that to him.

'You know, Krista, many's the time I've said it to you, if you're ever in trouble, you can come talk to your mother. Anything at all'.

'I know, mum'.

'But this time, all I can do is listen and advise. I think you should think seriously about taking your husband up on his offer'.

Krista said nothing. Sylvia got up and put a record on the stereo. It was an old Chet Baker album.

As he sang 'Look For The Silver Lining', Krista and Sylvia shared a companionable few minutes without speaking.

'Mum', Krista asked when the track ended. 'Do you think you're going to need hospice care?'

Sylvia regarded her daughter calmly, though her voice was still loud. 'Go to London. We can't have you giving up your life to look after an old crone like me'.

'But I will look after you'. Krista meant it.

'I would feel better not going through the humiliation of it'.

'You're not being appropriately sentimental, mum'.

'Remember when Sol got sick?' Sylvia said.

'Mum, I hope you're not reminding me that I pretty much fucked up with Dad'.

'I don't want you going through that. Wiping his arse, and so on'.

'Well then', Krista said. 'If you're going to a hospice, we have to find one that's right'.

'Don't you be worrying yourself', Sylvia said. 'The place in Harold's Cross will be grand'.

Episode IV

They had taken a small table near the door. Raimi was thankful for the breeze. This bar, called Blood, was full of business-suited men and women, most of them unaccustomed to smiling in public. Their hostess came to jot down their orders. She wore a crimson velvet dress and had her face painted deathly white, strikingly framed by Morticia Addams hair. It seemed to Raimi that Blood was trying too hard, an overdone place for the times that were in it. He had a feeling that it would not be open for much longer.

For all that, he was in need of refreshment after a morning spent editing a new propaganda film. RTÉ was showing them around the clock now and the airtime had to be fed. You couldn't have a blank screen. It was, as Bellingham had it, the only sin in television. Nice work if you could get it. Raimi was supposed to feel lucky.

Krista wasn't hungry so she had a glass of Red Ochre '17. Raimi took her lead and treated himself to a Saint Aubin '18.

'We need to start spending the money so we know it's ours', Krista said.

'That's one way of looking at it'.

'Mum has made up her mind. She's going to the hospice', Krista said.

'That explains your need for expensive wine. It's not about the money. You're bracing yourself for taking her to her final resting place. I'll come with. Is she leaving you her flat?'

'Fuck you, Raimi. She won't even let me take her, that's how stubborn she is'.

'Talk about Irish Mother syndrome. I'll be all right here in the dark'.

'And fuck you for what you just said about her flat'. Krista sighed.

'Sorry'.

Krista gave him a hard stare. 'She said you have to learn how to die in order to know how to live. Whatever the hell that means'.

'Well I'm sure they'll let you come and see her when you want to'.

'They might, but she won't'.

'She'll be denying herself as well as you'.

'I know'. Krista swirled the wine around her glass and sniffed it before sipping. 'I think she's afraid of being seen like that. Whatever it is they do to them. I don't think she really knows what to expect'.

'Maybe she does'.

'I'm going to miss her, Raimi'.

Raimi watched through the window as a brace of Specials sauntered by. A news item caught his attention.

The Shoga said, 'Plans for an elevator into space received a shot in the arm today as Congress approved funding'.

'Let's go to Mars', Raimi said, 'but first I have to get back to work'.

The documentary began with a profile of Joseph Walker, the Thalidomide Taoiseach. Compiled from news archives and interviews, the film described the now elderly Walker's upbringing and the path he had taken to his current success. There followed a profile of the PCP, which Walker founded after his falling out with Sinn Féin, his old party. The next segment recapitulated Ireland's Second Movement away from secularism, beginning with the first abortion and divorce referenda in the 1980s and 1990s. Then came the tale of a teenage girl giving birth alone in a grotto; she was presented as a martyr. After that was the story of a young woman held in custody by the Gardaí on behalf of the Director of Public Prosecutions, to prevent her travelling abroad for a termination; the Gardaí were the heroes now. Eventually, through economic and political shifts over decades, and even through periods when it appeared to be in the ascendant, the liberal agenda was finally defeated and the Progressive Christian Party rose to power on a wave of popular support. The Catholic Hierarchy, now a resurgent force, was assumed to approve of the Party. Indeed, the Church hardly ever pronounced these days on public and private morality. It didn't need to, because most people agreed with it. Raimi took in the history lesson with dismay, which he felt all the stronger as the documentary ended on a series of vox pops from ordinary citizens who had voted for the PCP in the recent election. Raimi had not voted.

'Things are better now', an expressionless man said on the screen.

'F.F. didn't go far enough', opined an old biddy.

'We don't want vagrants fouling up our streets', a teacher said. 'That's one of the things Walker gets right'.

'Blasphemy is a Christ-killer'. This was Kookaburra Stout, a young socialite regularly to be seen semi-naked in the pages of *Howya!*

Raimi spent several more hours on this edit. He had to take it, all this horror. He had to do it because it was his job. Not only that, this was his first solo run as a senior editor. Bellingham had stayed away deliberately to give him his head. Although the effect of the wine should have worn off, he still felt drunk.

'Coffee to Edit One, please', Raimi called into the mic. 'I so deserve it'.

Krista decided to see how Damo was settling in at The Foggy Dew. She had always liked the Foggy and she reckoned it was a better fit for him than his old job with her had been.

By the time she got to Fownes Street it was raining lightly and the smell of the Liffey had started to hurt her nostrils. At the pub door she saw a notice that the place was closed for Holy Hour. Krista had never seen a pub shut for that reason. Holy Hour was a dead custom, instituted by some stark, raving bishop back in the mists of time, and long abandoned. Now here it was again. She knocked on the door but there was no answer. She walked around to a window and tapped on it but still there was no response. There were lights on inside, however.

Krista took out her phone and dialled. A face appeared on the screen.

'Yeah, hi, Damo, this is …'

'Where are you?'

'Just outside. Can I talk to you for a minute?'

'Give me a moment'.

Krista clicked off, replaced the phone in her pocket and waited. The door opened and Damo limped out. He leaned against the wall.

'Krista'. He held out his hand and they shook.

'How are you?'

Damo looked at her with expectation; he knew she wanted something. 'Let's go'.

They walked further into Temple Bar.

'I'm opening a new place', Krista said. 'It's going to be slightly shady and I want you to run it'.

'Will it get us into bother?'

'Probably'.

'I'll think about it'.

'Thanks. You know people who could help. In return, I want you to be my business partner'.

Damo whistled. 'So where did you get the money?'

'My mother left it to me'.

'My mother never had any money'.

Temple Bar, with its boarded-up galleries and closed-down bookshops, usually made Krista feel sad. The cinema was still there, as were many of the bars, including the Matt Talbot of course, but other uses had been found for the derelict art-houses, the abandoned strip joints. The Temple Bar pub itself was now a candle emporium. As they passed it, Krista was reminded of her mother. Sylvia had told her of a time before gentrification when you could sit outside on the street, drinking a warm pint, enjoying the sunshine.

'Have you eaten?' Krista asked.

'No'.

They left the district behind and crossed the river to Liffey Street. There the Well Woman Centre hid behind an unmarked door. The statue of the two ladies sitting on a bench with their shopping, had long ago been replaced by a *Simpsons* pietà in bronze that the authorities had not yet got around to removing: Marge held a naked Homer across her lap in a Christlike pose, the kids at her feet like underachieving cherubim.

'Damo, why do you have a Holy Hour in the Foggy?'

'After the law did me over, we have to make sure we pay attention'.

'They missed your face. That's something'. Krista realised that she hadn't asked him if he was able to walk this far. Damo had done so anyway.

Minutes later they waited for service at a table in Pizza the Hutt. There were not many customers but the staff all seemed busy.

'I need you to make a contact for me, Damo', Krista said. She sized up the picture of a Quattro Staggione on the menu. 'In case we ever do need to get out, it'd help to have friends like yours'.

'And what do I get out of all this?'

'If it comes to it and you help us leave, you get the new bar'.

Damo did not appear to be listening as he scanned the menu. He was going to have a Nettuno and Krista was paying. 'Tell me what you need', he said, after a moment.

Raimi's latest propaganda documentary, an anti-abortion flick, was called *The Christ Inside*. Unless he censored the whole thing, he thought, there was no way to cut this picture without making himself sick. Bellingham, sitting in on the edit just to be sociable, did not seem to mind.

'When I came here first from the mainland', he said, 'this digital stuff was in its infancy. None of you young whippersnappers have any appreciation of what it was like to work with real film. Oh, those were great days'.

'Young people today. We don't know we're born', Raimi said.

The morning had started with doughnuts and coffee. They checked out the files that had come in, and had selected scenes to match the script that the Department had supplied. Why they needed editors at all, Raimi did not know. There was no choosing involved. Maybe they just liked paying people to do their bidding.

Raimi's stomach was finding it tough to stay put. He had already seen short passages of graphic violence being done to abortion workers: a clinic in Florida bombed; a doctor in London taken out into the street and shot; a nurse in Milan raped and dismembered in the name of Jesus. Each atrocity was sanctioned by a different passage in the Bible, to be titled onscreen where appropriate.

Raimi tuned in to the voiceover to try and detect any trace of irony but so far had found none.

'Where do we draw the line in our efforts to protect the unborn?' the voice said. 'Do we say that those who perform Satan's butchery deserve to live? Or do we eradicate these evildoers?'

Suddenly there began secret footage of an abortion being carried out. Raimi's stomach finally lurched.

'I can't watch this', Raimi said.

'Come on. This is kids' stuff'. Bellingham sounded pleased at the young man's discomfort.

'Back in a moment'. Raimi left Edit One and hurtled to the bathroom down the hall. He barely made it before throwing up into the bowl.

When he returned, Raimi found Bellingham at the desk, joyfully taking over the edit. The older man was now scanning footage of a drugged doctor tied to a mechanical cross which was laid flat on the ground in the yard of Mountjoy prison. With his arms missing, two leather straps bound the doctor across his chest and ankles. The voiceover ran on: '... finally accepts full responsibility for what he has done and is sentenced to C&D, or crucifixion and dismemberment. His profile will now be added to the Register of Criminals'.

Raimi sat down, his face still pale.

Powered by hydraulic pistons, the cross on the screen began to rise.

'Are you ok?' Bellingham asked. 'You're white as a nun's tampon'.

'Bellingham, I have a serious question here. Can we work on something a little less despicable? You know, like an Auschwitz Glee Club home heating demonstration'.

'Sure, sure', Bellingham changed his tone. 'You need some weak tea'.

'I think I need a holiday', Raimi said. 'In Somalia'.

'Oh come on, son. It's not like we're doing anything we couldn't take home and show the wife ...'

'It's exactly like that'. Raimi wanted to spit.

'My missus wouldn't find this stuff objectionable'.

'Your missus?'

'Maura is old-school'.

Raimi got up again and stood by the wall. Sitting had given him the anticipation of a projectile moment. 'I'll be all right in a minute'.

'Well', Bellingham said, 'let's take a break anyway. You remember that list of dirty films you asked me about?'

'Seriously?'

'I won't say a word. Come along with uncle Reg and let me show you the secrets of cinema'.

A moment later, in a back room beyond Elaine's office, Bellingham hunched down beside a low filing cabinet that stood against one wall, as Raimi looked on. Bellingham heaved his shoulder against the cabinet and moved it away to reveal a gap in the floorboards.

'Down here', Bellingham said. He lifted a loose board, set it aside and reached into the dark. Then he pulled up a small box.

'How's about that then?' Bellingham handed the box to Raimi, replaced the floorboard then moved the cabinet back.

Raimi opened the lid of the box. Inside he saw eight disc cases. He pulled one out. '*From Dusk Till Dawn*'.

'Banned here', Bellingham smirked. 'Would you believe it?'

Raimi scanned the rest: '*E.T. the Extra* – God I haven't seen that one in ages'.

'Banned here, now'.

'*It's A Wonderful Life*'.

'Banned'. Bellingham took the case from Raimi.

'Why don't you come over one night next week? We could watch it then'.

'Sounds like a plan. Now let's get back to work'. Bellingham walked past Raimi and out into the hall.

'Where did you get these?'

Bellingham didn't look back as he entered Edit One. 'My own personal stash', he said.

Raimi followed him into the suite and closed the door. He set the box on the console then sat down. Bellingham landed on the couch, still holding *It's A Wonderful Life*. 'You know we could be jailed for this'.

'We?'

'Yeah, but it doesn't matter, because nobody's going to find out'.

Raimi took the rest of the discs out of the box and laid them on the desk to inspect them. *From Dusk Till Dawn*.

Blade Runner. E.T. the Extra-Terrestrial. The Exorcist. The Last Temptation of Christ. The Matrix. Dune.

'These films all have religious subjects', Raimi said. 'They're all on the Index'. He felt elated rather than scared. 'Bellingham, this is hot stuff'.

'You asked if I could get you some shady movies, I got you some shady movies. I just hope you know what you're doing'.

'Lucky we don't have *Lolita*. Even the film is jailbait now'.

The screen began to move again. Raimi leaned back in his chair and his elbow brushed against a button. The film skipped to the next scene, one which they had not yet edited. Music started up: the percussive finalé to Part One of Mike Oldfield's *Ommadawn*.

Then he saw the footage that the music accompanied.

Eight pro-choice agitators, chained together, faced a firing squad in the yard of Mountjoy. As one was shot and fell, the others felt her weight tugging on the rope. The executioners fired at random so that the prisoners did not know which of them would be next, each execution a heart-stopping surprise for all of them. *Bang*. Finally the last of the eight fell. The cohort of protesters lay on top of each other, still tied together, some of them twitching. One of the officers walked over to a woman who was still breathing, and shot her in the head with his revolver.

Raimi and Bellingham sat, both riveted. The scene ended, to be replaced by the Thalidomide Christ logo of the PCP.

'We're not working on that', Raimi said. 'I've had it. We're not putting that shit out for broadcast'.

'Not putting what out for broadcast?' Elaine Brooks had entered the room quietly while the two men were watching the display.

'That's ob-shitting-scene', Bellingham said, mocking Raimi. 'An ob-shitting-scene scene'.

Elaine Brooks did not laugh at Bellingham's joke. She had spotted the discs, stalked over and picked up *Blade Runner*. 'What are you doing with these?'

Raimi put on an innocent face. '*Blade Runner*. Good film. Lovely art direction'.

'I want an explanation'.

On the screen the Thalidomide Christ flickered. None of them was watching it now.

'My fault, Elaine', Bellingham said. 'I found them'.

'Found them?'

'In the stock room. They've been here for years. Old as the hills'.

'You didn't bring them in?'

'No'.

'Must've been here when we moved in', Elaine conceded. 'I want them gone, ok? I won't have the company compromised again'.

Then she made to leave.

'Elaine', Raimi said.

Elaine turned around.

'What did you come in here for?'

'Oh. I just wanted to know how the documentary is coming along. We have a meeting at five'.

'The documentary is fine', Bellingham said. 'It's obscene'.

'... Deploring the incident, Minister O'Toole yesterday announced the setting-up of a new Bureau of Deportation to deal with refugees ...'

Raimi turned from the Airtram TV and looked across the water at the converted oil platform, wondering at how those illegal immigrants lived in their cages out there, like so many battery hens.

The movies were in his backpack. He was sure that he looked self-conscious and he feared a random inspection. At Blackrock, nobody stopped him. Even the ticketmaster at the station appeared not to notice him or his contraband. There were too many people passing through this evening on account of what appeared to be a massive prayer meeting in the park. Raimi had not heard it announced and had not expected the park to be so packed. It meant that he did not stand out.

'What's up?' Raimi asked a fellow passenger on disembarking. 'Prayer service?'

'You could say that', the other man answered. 'Hurling match'.

Krista wore a red party dress. Her hair was burnt sienna. Two crimson court shoes stood on the floor beside her in the living room.

'You look nice', Raimi said when he came in. 'And red'.

'I thought we could go to Mass this evening'. Krista picked up the shoes but did not put them on. She turned to see him, her man-child.

'Why on earth would we go to Mass?'

'To pray for Mum. We're going to bring her in tomorrow'.

'Already? Oh, Krista'. He stepped back against the wall.

'You'll come with us?'

'I will'. Raimi reflected on the weight of a life.

'Thank you'.

'But I can't go to Mass', he said, 'It stinks of bad dentistry'.

Krista picked up a shoe and threw it at him.

'Ow!' The shoe bounced on his chest.

'Show some respect'.

'You go. I'm watching a movie'. He took his backpack off and opened it.

'Movie?'

'You won't believe what'. Raimi got the box of films out of his backpack. 'Something I haven't seen in years'.

She seemed uninterested. 'Can I have my shoe back?'

'Check these out first'. He dropped the bag and approached her with the films.

'You don't have to come to Mass', Krista said. 'Stay here and watch your little film if you want'.

'Seriously?'

'It's a free country'. She came over and kissed him on the forehead, taking his box of films as she did so. Krista flipped through the discs. 'Are these banned?'

'Most of them'.

'I think all of them are'. Krista held one of the cases up to the evening light. 'What do you get for *E.T.*?'

'I don't know. A SIM card?'

'Ten years'. Krista hit Raimi on the head with the case of *E.T. the Extra-Terrestrial* then handed the entire box of films back. 'Damo's working on our dispensation'.

'How can we be rebellious if we've got permission?' Raimi put the films down on the bed.

'Who said anything about being rebellious?' Krista huffed just a little.

'You did'.

'Oh'.

'And Krista, tell me this. Why are you going out dressed like the child bride of a Gonzaga boy?'

'You're such a wit, Raimi. Don't worry about me. I'll be back in a couple of hours. Then I want you to fuck me gently with a chainsaw'.

'A chainsaw'.

'Wrapped in fur'.

When she had gone, Raimi slipped *Blade Runner* in the TV. He found that he loved it even more for knowing that he had a copy.

Los Angeles, November 2019.

Blade Runner was better than any *Star Wars* film, no question. It was better than *Dark City*. It was even better than *Twelve Monkeys*.

Had anyone asked, Raimi would have sworn that he had always known Deckard was a replicant. You could see it in his eyes. You could guess from the way Gaff said, 'You've done a man's job, sir!' You could tell by the way Ridley Scott had once confirmed it in an interview.

As he watched he became enchanted again by its stygian landscape, its Syd Mead future that was now so far in the past.

Batty wanted more life. 'Fucker'.

Didn't we all?

Raimi regretted that there was no more blow left. What had possessed Krista to make her go to Mass? Her mum was about to enter the hospice. That could be it.

The hospice was known as 'Hotel California'. He had read up on it and thought it sounded like a not bad place in which to shuffle off. The staff made your last days bearable by drugging your food. When it was finally time to go gentle into that good night, you were given a meal laced with a slow-acting poison. You were not told which meal it was: breakfast, lunch or dinner. The drug was timed to carry you off painlessly at some point in the near future. At the hospice, unlike the establishment in the Charlton Heston movie, you did not get to watch films of bucolic paradises masquerading as the afterlife. You were shown Buster Keaton movies, Chaplin films, Harold Lloyd shorts – to remind you of how absurd life could be, and how lucky you were to be leaving it.

Episode V

There was one feature of her new bar that Krista would not be changing. The estate agents had painted over the Sistine-Chapel-inspired ceiling on the first floor but traces showed through, a palimpsest effect that pleased her. In a design based on an old postcard, this pastiche of *The Creation of Adam* was quite blasphemous, the first man in the Bible having been replaced by Bart Simpson. Krista felt a small thrill to know that it was hidden there. Inspired by the concealed picture, she had recently masturbated in the loo while picturing Michelangelo's deity pointing a finger at her, Palpatine lightning coruscating from its tip like an ejaculation of photons. That time, she wondered if God actually had fingerprints and if not, how they would recognise his corpse. Dental records?

They might soon find out. The government had recently commissioned UCD to conduct cloning experiments intended to capture some of the Messiah's qualities without actually resurrecting him. Clearly there was a line they would not cross. According to the *Times,* a cutting from the Shroud of Turin, on loan from the Vatican, had yielded the required biological matter. The Progressive Christians, disregarding the carbon dating that had established the Shroud's temporal provenance as the late Middle Ages, wished to retrieve the DNA of their Saviour from the fragment. Krista wondered why they would want to do such a thing, and how they could reconcile it with their ban on using stem cells. 'The Great Experiment', the news had called it but it seemed to Krista to be a great delusion. Someone in power was wrong in the head.

Formally the bar was called La Ville-Lumière. That's what the sign over the entrance said. Krista had already taken to abbreviating that to 'Lumière'. It stood in Blackrock a few doors from O'Rourke's. On the ground floor it was a narrow warren of snugs. The upstairs was open plan, a bar at one end and a big blank wall at the other. There were no seats yet but there would be – cinema seats. The official opening of the Banned-Film Club, to be held at the bar, was weeks away. The thought of it made her giddy.

Two months earlier, Damo had left the Foggy to join Krista in setting up Lumière. She was paying him out of Sylvia's bequest – a small retainer for now. They would need other staff as well of course, but had not yet hired anyone. Raimi thought her crazy to buy this place instead of using Sylvia's money to get them out of the country. Lumière was another strong tie, which made it harder for them to leave.

Bellingham seemed glad to give a good home to some film paraphernalia a mate of his had gathering dust in a back room in Chapelizod. Adding to their store of other people's stardust memories, Raimi had found a decorative projector in an antiques shop. It didn't work but would blend well with the items Bellingham had brought: a moviola, a telecine machine, a broken popcorn-maker, framed lobby cards from the 1980s, and a mannequin dressed as an usherette with her tray of cigarette packets. Along the walls in the upstairs bar, hung posters of classic films: *Betty Blue, Vertigo, His Girl Friday, A Man of No Importance* and others. One of these was a beautiful black and white poster for *Manhattan* that Krista had bought from Barnes & Noble. She had also purchased a cardboard standee of R2-D2 as a present for Raimi, and placed it in one corner of the room, under the space where the screen would be.

Damo had managed to get a provisional viewing licence from his contact in the Department. This allowed them, he told Krista, to show each film once in public to a non-paying audience, as an educational exercise. Private viewings, he assured her, did not need official approval.

The inaugural meeting of The Banned-Film Club, on the first Tuesday in August, was to be a dry run. The bar was closed for the occasion, a 'private party' sign on the front door. Bellingham sat beside the digital projector at the bar. All around, the film-world souvenirs imbued the place with what Krista felt was a special atmosphere, as might be encountered in a hidden corner of Kane's warehouse. Raimi, on the other hand, worried that all this stuff might be mere tat, fit for a charity shop.

A large red velvet couch like an oversized love seat, squatted in the middle of the floor facing the wall. In front of it sat a low table for their drinks and shop-bought popcorn.

Krista took her glass of wine then stood up, her back to the screen.

'I'd like to thank you all for the hard work you've put in over the last few weeks, getting this place together. Raimi, for banging in the nails, Damo for the legal stuff, and Reg for the wonderful memorabilia and the films themselves. Now a toast'. She raised her glass. 'To Sylvia. Without her gift, The Banned-Film Club would not be possible'.

They clinked and sipped, all but Bellingham who, though he lifted his glass, did not drink from it.

'Lights', Krista said.

Damo hurried over to the switch by the stairwell, turned out the lights and sat down. When everyone else had settled in the dark, Bellingham pressed play then joined them.

A bell tolled and the title, *Liberty Films presents* appeared over it. This was quickly replaced by a still-frame illustration of two people in a horse-drawn buggy riding in a snowy landscape. Now the titles flipped in a series of cards removed by hand. Two minutes in, there was a conference in heaven. Clarence the Angel was called upon to go down to earth, and the story of George Bailey began to play out.

Later, as far as Raimi was concerned, was when it got interesting.

George Bailey staggers drunkenly onto a bridge. It is Christmas. It is snowing. It is the end of the world. Bailey wonders how the devil he got himself into this mess. The answer is simple: he helped people out. He forsook his ambition to travel the world, his desire to break free of the bonds of small-town life, his unwillingness to let others shoulder their own burdens. He's a hero but nobody thanks him for it: not his uncle, not his brother, not Mr Potter. Nobody can tell him what he might have found in those far-off places he will never see. No one can show him the path not taken. For now, Bailey is thinking: end it. He will jump off this bridge, negate all of his unfulfilled ambitions, blank out his own existence. He will rekindle his dampened spirit of adventure by leaping prematurely into the greatest adventure of all. But what goes on? Who is that big, dumb-looking guy with the damn fool smile and the outsize overcoat? Who asked him to stick his nose in where it's not wanted?

It's an angel who has to earn his wings. That's who it is. Here comes the angel.

'Here comes the angel', Raimi said. 'I bet he ruins things'.

'Oh, come off it', Bellingham said. 'Clarence is the best thing in this film. He needs this mission, doesn't he? Gives him a reason to live. You know what they say about an angel in heaven'.

'No I don't. Shush'. That was Krista, with a dirty look.

'You've seen this one before', Raimi said to Bellingham.

The film rolled on, drawing these watchers deeper into its world of alternative realities. One of the greatest fantasy films he'd ever seen, and it was about ordinary people, Raimi thought. Who knew that reality could have so much crazy shit in it?

'I love the wife', Krista said later. 'She's so passive aggressive. Why didn't you ever throw a lasso around the moon for me, Raimi?'

'You wouldn't have noticed'.

'True'.

'Well, I like it', Bellingham said. 'I like its innocence. I wonder why this one's on the Index'.

'Unrealistic depiction of celestial beings', Damo surmised.

Bellingham said, 'I think it's a shame films like this had to go. I mean …'

'Shh', said Raimi.

'I would have liked Evil Bedford Falls', Krista said.

'Without this film, we'd have no *Simpsons*', Damo said.

'What do you mean?' Bellingham asked. 'No *Simpsons*'.

'C. Montgomery Burns. Love child of Nosferatu and Mr Potter', Raimi said.

'Shut up', Krista said. 'This is a heartwarming film. Ok?'

'It isn't', Raimi countered.

'Sorry?'

'Its message is that men are dispensable', Raimi said. 'At least that's what I get from this first viewing. Men are disposable; family men, doubly so'.

'You stupid tit', Krista said. 'It's a bloody comedy. Have you been at the "Wankers for Justice" pills again?'

'Now Raimi', Bellingham chipped in. 'I think you can see this film as anti-family in general'.

'The cult of the male as worker ant', Raimi said, glaring at Krista. 'That's not anti-family'.

'I think it's a queer love story', Damo said. 'Clarence obviously is nuts about George'.

'You're kidding me'. Krista saw his point but felt it was not what Capra had meant.

'Think about it. When George gets to heaven, Clarence will be waiting for him, wings outstretched. It's obvious, isn't it? Clarence is the one who's frustrated'.

'You're possibly right', she said. 'Now let's watch the cocksucking film'.

They piped down and surrendered to the bittersweet magic. During the rest of the film, no one said anything. Then the movie was over and Bailey was saved, more or less.

'That was great', Raimi said.

'I really rather enjoyed that', Bellingham said, getting up, 'but now I must hit the road'.

'No problem', Krista said. She rose and took the glasses. She looked around to see if Raimi was still angry with women. He might very well have forgotten his outburst already.

Bellingham sniffed the air as he took the disc out of the projector and placed it back in its case. 'In my day, they used to ban things like *A Clockwork Orange*'.

'That was never banned', Raimi said. 'Kubrick pulled it'.

'No', Bellingham said. 'Here it was banned'.

Damo walked over to the bar. 'Krista, everybody, I'll be off. Cheers for a grand evening. See you tomorrow'.

'Night', Raimi said.

'Wait a bit', Bellingham said. 'Give you a lift'.

'Hey, thanks'.

Bellingham handed the film to Raimi. 'Put this somewhere safe'.

Krista saw the two men out. The street was quiet. Not many people were about on a Tuesday.

They slept on the couch that night but didn't fuck. Krista brought a glass of wine to the table for herself in case she couldn't nod off, and dropped half a pill to make sure that she would. Raimi took nothing to either elevate or deflate his mood. He was tired.

The iron sea air wafted in through the open window. Although they could not see the moon from where they lay, its light cast a projector's beam in reverse on the floor, making a shadow film in which Krista and Raimi were both players and screen. He felt insubstantial in that light. She didn't notice any effect on herself.

Krista curled into his body. 'Are we asking for trouble?'

'Your friend got us a licence'.

'Oh but who knows about that. I've made a plan anyway'. Krista turned around in his embrace, high on her own sense of occasion. 'Damo's had a word with his guy in Chernobyltown'.

Back at the flat the next morning, Krista took a shower. She daydreamed that she was in an art gallery where all of the faces in all of the pictures had melted into one many-rooted snake of paint composed of elongated sourpuss El Greco martyrs, naked dryads, armour-plated knights and supplicant apostles. The snake had itself a face: the sombre physiognomy of Christ. He kissed her, this refugee from a

Garden of Eden twinned with Golgotha; he kissed her and there were tongues. During her fantasy, Krista experienced what she later considered her first religious orgasm, despite those she'd enjoyed while picturing God as the Sith Emperor Palpatine. When she came to, she was holding the showerhead upside-down between her thighs, spraying hot needles. Out of her dream, Krista smiled. She didn't know why, but she felt that everything would be all right, that something wonderful was going to happen.

Episode VI

It had been Krista's idea to see the play about the Legion and Raimi had gone along with it. Afterwards, in the bar of the Abbey, he suggested that the Legionnaires might be like the Jedi, who had started off as humble galactic policemen protecting the Old Republic against evil, but had become too self-important, so that the Sith were given a red carpet.

'The Jedi', Krista said, 'are not real'.

'I'm not going to argue with you about that', Raimi said. 'But why did you bring us to this stupid play anyway?'

'I thought it looked interesting'.

'Let's go'.

For the sake of a walk, they ambled along the quays to Temple Bar. At Curved Street they spotted a new Transgression Booth on the corner with Eustace Street. These pop-up confessionals had been appearing on streets throughout the city. The idea was that you went in and made your admissions of guilt to a receiver that identified your voice pattern and issued you with instructions on which prayers to recite in penance. At some unspecified time in the future, you might receive a visit from the

Specials, who would take you to a police station for interrogation. That was how the propaganda film told it. There was no guarantee that you would ever be arrested, but if you were, you could end up in front of the Provisional Tribunal at Dublin Castle. There were worse places you could find yourself, but not many.

'I don't fancy our chances in that', Raimi said.

They rounded the corner.

'Holy shit', Krista shrieked. 'My bar!'

The Matt Talbot was gone. A new building stood in its place. In darkness the edifice seemed to melt into the sky. It was an ugly obsidian tower with one large window two floors up, above a huge door that gave the impression of being impenetrable. A sign in black relief over the door read: *Seminary Twelve: A UCD Facility*. Half-way down the door they saw the logo: a foot-square reproduction of the face from the Shroud of Turin. Raimi was reminded of what nightclubs used to look like.

Krista staggered back a little, to take in the whole of the structure. She glanced at the sign then at the logo. 'This', she said, 'is a Seminary'.

'A semi what?'

'A Seminary replaces my old bar and no one tells me'.

Raimi felt fury rise in his chest. He wanted to smash the building and didn't know why. There was something plain wrong about this thing, this black monolith of hate.

'Let's just go', Krista said.

Raimi held his anger down as she dragged him away.

'What's a Seminary?' he asked as they went.

'A facility where they clone priests'.

'You've got to be joking'. Raimi pulled his hand out of Krista's grip and ran over to the black building. He stopped in front of the door and unzipped his trousers.

'What the hell are you doing?'

As if his cock shared his rage Raimi pissed without apparent effort. He gushed a great arc on the Seminary door, spraying the metal, signing his name in some personal ritual. Then he aimed directly at the picture of the Shroud detail in the door, soaking it so that the face wept.

Krista watched him go. It was too ridiculous. She laughed raucously then rushed to him and tugged at his arm as he shook the last falling drops.

'You didn't drink that much in the bar', she said. 'Where did all that piss come from?'

The alarm sounded. Raimi had tripped a laser.

He zipped up.

Krista and Raimi whirled away, laughing, but he couldn't resist punching the Transgression Booth on the corner of the street as they went.

Krista pulled him away again.

The Transgression Booth came to life. A light went on and a grinding of machinery started up.

'Citizen', the Booth said. 'Please maintain your position and prepare to be interviewed'.

'The fuck!'

Raimi glared at the Booth but Krista was already turning the corner. Seeing her flee, he legged it after her. They dodged up Eustace Street and on to Dame Street then slowed to a walk and hailed an oncoming cab that looked empty.

'Christ!' Krista swore, as the taxi pulled in. 'I can't believe you just did that'.

'This Seminary ...' Raimi said.

Bellingham looked up. He was archiving some files at a console. Raimi flipped through random pages on his own screen.

'Some bugger deposits the wrong stuff on the wrong side of the door. You have to laugh. Poor Jesus gets a soaking'.

'Well, what is a Seminary? They don't tell you on the news'.

'Breeding unit for priests'.

'You're kidding. What's wrong with growing them in Maynooth from emotionally retarded youths like they used to?'

'Just a sec …' Bellingham copied some files over to the backup drive. 'For one thing, they reckon anyone who's had a life before becoming a priest is going to have baggage, don't you know, and I can see their logic. These new ones will only be born with original sin, absolved through baptism. That's a pretty simple fix. Give me the child and I'll show you the man, like the Jesuits used to say'.

'Give me the child and I'll show you a porno'.

'Anyway, it doesn't concern us', Bellingham said. 'You're not likely to want a job as a dispenser of the sacraments, eh? You're not from the right stock'.

'Bellingham, you're a racist dick'.

'I thought you were Irish. Anyway, they want fresh material. They get the sperm from specially screened volunteers'.

'Yeah but that doesn't answer the most obvious question'.

'Which is?'

'Where do they get the eggs?'

The Airtram moved out and scraped all the way to Pearse before the sound settled down. Approaching Aviva, the tram shuddered to a halt and the 'Doors Locked' sign came on.

A news bulletin interrupted the commercials. According to the Shoga, a car bomb had just hit New Liberty Hall.

The tram must have been too far away for him to hear the blast. Raimi immediately pegged the culprit as an architect. The Specials still hadn't worked out a body count. Perhaps hundreds of office workers had been caught in the blast; or only a few cleaning staff. There was too much rubble. The hazard crews had not started bringing out the bodies.

It took seconds for people to turn away, impatient for their journey to resume. But Raimi focused on the screen. He felt as if he recognised the components of the explosion suspended in a moment of time, long after they had fallen away into no space at all.

Krista had predicted it would be a busy night. Raimi had half a mind to go over to Lumière and take a drink with her. Instead he took a shower and sat to dry in front of the TV. There was a show on RTÉ about hamsters. Flicking through the channels, he found nothing about the car bomb, so he switched back to the national broadcaster and settled down.

A woman talked to camera, recounting a story from her youth. One day she came in from an errand and found her hamster, Bertie, lying dead in his cage, his tiny paws up in the air, his eyes shut tight in little crosses. As her sisters were out on a shopping trip with her mother, she was alone in the house. Tenderly removing Bertie from his cage, she kissed him on the nose and placed him in an old shoebox that she found under the sink. She covered him over with sawdust from his cage. She put his wheel in with him and closed the shoebox. This she took out into the yard behind the farmhouse, a graveyard for old, broken-down machinery. There was a patch of soil at the end of the yard and no one had grown vegetables in it for years. It was overrun with weeds. She brought the shoebox out there, got down on her knees and with her bare hands dug a grave for the hamster. Years later, when she told this story to her husband, he said something that put he heart crossways inside her: hamsters hibernate. She had buried poor Bertie alive, and the guilt of it nearly killed her.

A title came on: *Remember this, next time you think of murdering a baby.*

'Jesus!' Raimi quickly changed the channel to BBC 4.

Fear of Fanny came on. Raimi always laughed at that title.

The phone rang and Krista's face appeared. 'Come over to the bar tonight, Raimi. I have a surprise for you'.

It was after curfew now. The day's business was done and the bar had been cleared. By the time Raimi arrived, Damo was washing glasses.

'It's *E.T.* tonight', Damo said as Raimi sat down at the bar.

Krista came up and hugged him.

'Did you hear the explosion?' he asked.

'Sorry?' Krista hadn't, obviously.

Damo put a vodka down and Raimi nodded acknowledgement. 'It was after I left. Rattled windows for miles, according to the Shoga'.

'I must have been in the shower'. She leaned over and kissed him. 'You're still an idiot'.

'That', Raimi said, 'I am'.

Krista looked at Damo. 'Can I get a gin, sir?'

Damo prepared a couple of gins, handed one to her and kept one for himself.

They were past tipsy when Bellingham arrived, apologising for his tardiness. His wife had wanted him to spend the evening with her.

Soon they were sitting on the couch upstairs, wine in front of them. The opening credits rolled.

'Shh …' Krista said as LA's illuminated grid spread out before them.

They watched without speaking. When E.T. resurrected, nobody sought to make the comparison with Christ. Similarly, when the little alien left Elliot to go home on his ship, no one likened it to the ascension. They all took *E.T.* for a straight-up allegory of Jesus. It was Spielberg's most devout work.

When the movie ended, Krista saw Bellingham and Damo to the door.

'Raimi, I have a bad feeling about this', she said on her return upstairs.

Raimi poured himself a vodka. 'We have a licence'.

'This club', Krista said. She grabbed his glass and sniffed it. 'I know we're not open to the public, but what if they bust us anyway?'

'Like it's a front for the Blackrock chapter of the Anglican Militia? Shit, we might as well bomb the Seminary and get some value out of it. That's ridiculous'. Raimi didn't mind that she had stolen his drink. 'If it makes you nervous, the Banned-Film Club is over, Krista. Lumière is just a bar'.

'Ok', she agreed without regret. 'That's settled then. We dump the discs'.

Episode VII

Krista and Raimi enjoyed a long couple of hours in bed, kissing and playing. Now he was up and about, still wearing his pyjamas, making breakfast in the kitchen. It was Krista's idea that they would take the day off work and visit Damo's contact in Chernobyltown. While he popped croissants into the oven and percolated Java, Raimi felt good in himself. Krista was deciding things today.

He brought the breakfast into the bedroom. Krista stretched and yawned. He put the tray down on the bed and got in beside her.

'It feels like we're bunking off school', he said.

'We have a history, Raimi', Krista said. The thought had just hit her. 'A Tweet for you, an old Facebook post for me. Nothing is ever deleted'.

'That's a bit of a heavy thought', Raimi said, 'and I was having such a nice day'.

'Still, it's true'. Krista picked up a croissant and bit into it, letting flakes shower down on her breast.

'How long have we been together now?' Raimi asked.

'A long time. Too long'.

'Let's just have breakfast and see how we get on', Raimi said.

After her shower, Krista wandered into the living room as the phone rang. She picked up the remote. A uniformed woman, obviously not a Shoga, appeared on the screen. She introduced herself.

'It is my duty to tell you', the woman said, 'that your mother passed away in the early hours'.

'Oh –'

'Sylvia Monica Wallace entered the next life gracefully, after a light supper of ravioli administered by Doctor Wong three days previously'.

Raimi sauntered in. He found Krista standing in her towel, holding the remote away from her body. She looked mislaid.

'The cremation service will be held here tomorrow', the woman on the screen said. 'I will g-mail the details along with your security passes'.

'Oh, Krista, I'm sorry', Raimi said. 'You poor –'

'You have my condolences'. The woman on the screen sounded like a cash register.

A Specials roadblock backed up the traffic at Ballsbridge. More drones than usual hovered above. Looking up out the window of the taxi, Raimi counted four. They must all be working different districts.

Krista sat in contemplation, her handbag in her lap. It had their passes in it, as well as their cash. She would need a lot of that today.

Raimi ventured an opinion. 'Liberty Hall Bombers'.

'What?' the driver said.

'Liberty Hall was hit by a car bomb'.

'You're joking'.

'Keep it down', Krista said.

The Specials waved the taxi through the checkpoint.

Minutes later the driver was speeding off towards Ranelagh and as the car turned, Krista glanced in the direction of New Mespil.

At Belgrave Square they joined a tailback. The traffic seemed denser than usual. There was a delay of some kind at the junction with Rathmines Road, where the lights were stuck on red. The driver said: 'Sorry about this, folks, but there's nothing I can do about whatever eejit is holding up the rest of us'.

The car turned at the lights and the driver pushed on towards Harold's Cross. A three-car pile-up had scattered metal and glass all along the road by the Esso station. An ambulance was on the scene. The police station opposite had sent three Specials out to assist the ambulance crew. Cars crawled past the wreckage. The Specials ignored the small crowd of rubberneckers who had gathered.

Krista averted her eyes so as not to see the carnage. Raimi gaped. It was his first car accident. A young woman, concussed and bleeding from the head, walked unsteadily as an ambulance worker led her away. The sirens were silent but the lights flashed. One Special helped another draw a police tape around the scene. Fuel spilled dangerously. The barbecue stench of burnt flesh filled the air and made Raimi feel peckish. A Special pulled a child out of one of the cars that had landed on its side. The kid's face was red with blood. This was not the kind of thing Krista should see on the way to her mother's cremation, Raimi thought. She must be feeling terrible. But it could be that the crash is good for her. Distracting.

'Are you ok?' he asked.

She said nothing. The car moved as fast as the traffic would allow, edging past the scene of the crash.

Raimi took one voyeuristic look through the back window and caught the eye of the C-Special who was rescuing the child. The cop was a young man with a kind face. Raimi smiled at him and the C-Special's expression changed in an instant. His brow furrowed as he put the child on the ground almost absentmindedly then stood up again looking like he had forgotten where he had put his hat. His purpose became clear when he pulled his gun out and aimed it at the taxi.

'Officer?' an ambulance worker called out.

The C-Special fired and the bullet shattered the rear window of the taxi before hitting the windscreen and cracking that.

Neither Raimi or Krista had time to understand what was happening. The driver howled and put his foot down. The taxi skidded sideways and mounted the pavement with a crunch of headlights. It smashed against a lamp post. Raimi and Krista spun to the right. Krista banged her head on the window. She was out, her body cushioning Raimi as he thumped against her like a retort.

The driver's airbag blew up. Recovering quickly, he deflated it then pulled the car into the road but the C-Special was already out in front, taking aim again as the rubberneckers dispersed and the ambulance workers scurried behind their vehicle.

The other cops started yelling now. Spotting the fuel on the road, one of them called out. 'Hold your fire!'

The cop with the gun ignored them and stalked towards the car, his weapon raised.

'What's he doing?' Raimi stared.

The Special commanded: 'Gerouhadafuckincar!'

'Culchie bastard!' the taxi driver shouted back. He didn't cut the engine but neither did he accelerate.

'Gerouhadafuckincar! All of yees'.

'All of yees?' The driver spat.

'Get us out of here!' Raimi shouted but they weren't moving.

'Sorry, fella', the driver said. 'Nothing I can do for you'.

His gun held high, the C-Special opened the door on Raimi's side and dragged him into the road. Raimi banged his head on the ground and curled up in pain. Krista was unconscious. The other Specials started to run for the taxi.

Raimi kicked at the C-Special but missed. The cop reached down and butted him on the head with his gun.

The driver saw the Specials racing for him and as Raimi yelled on the ground, the taxi abandoned him, screeching away.

Krista came to. She saw what was happening and made herself small in the back seat.

The cop who had taken Raimi, fired after the taxi again. This time he missed. 'Bastarding shite!'

The taxi was gone. The other C-Specials stood around to watch as their colleague turned his attention back to Raimi, reaching down and lifting him off the ground. The confused young man could hardly stand.

'Up agin the wall!' the C-Special barked, indicating with his gun the window of the Despar shop.

'It's a window!' Raimi staggered over to it, watched by the cops.

'Hands up'.

The ambulance crew had emerged from their cover. 'Give us a hand here', one said and the C-Specials ignored them.

The cop frisked Raimi. 'Where were ye going?'

'To a funeral'. Raimi was barely able to speak. Pain split his skull.

'Someone close was it?'

'My almost mother-in-law'.

'Sorry for yeer trouble. But I have here a identification that fits your description'. He poked Raimi with his gun. 'Turn around, slow, like'.

Raimi turned around. 'What have I done?'

'I have here a identification'. He showed Raimi the image on his wrist screen. It was the digital photograph the empty kid had taken in O'Brien's.

Then came a lance of electricity that cut through him and made him fall unconscious to the ground. Someone had Tased him remotely.

Krista had passed out again. Now she came to on the side of the road at Butterfield Close where the driver had dumped her. He was already pulling away. She shouted after him. 'Raimi!'

She was surprised when the driver braked then reversed to where she was gathering herself off the ground. At least she still had her handbag. The driver had left her with that. Standing now, Krista yelled. 'What the fuck just happened?'

The driver did not get out but his voice was loud enough for her to hear. 'The cops took your man. I'm sorry but there's nothing I can do'.

'You made me leave him'.

'I wouldn't go to the hospice if I were you. And as for your man, forget him. He's dead'.

'Take me back!'

'I'm doing you a favour, love'.

'Fuck you'.

'Ah, fuck yourself. And who's gonna pay for my windows? You answer me that'. The man shook his head in disgust then turned away.

The engine coughed and the car wheezed off but it didn't get far. Two hundred yards down the road, it burst into flames.

Krista threw herself into a garden and hid. She peered out at the burning taxi. Above it a drone descended vertically to inspect the damage. She ducked down behind the garden wall. Only when she heard the drone moving away, did she dare expose her presence again. She looked out on the road. Some children had come to warm themselves at the inferno that the taxi had made. The flesh of the driver on fire turned the air black around the cab. The children copped this and first one, then the others, ran away screaming. Krista thought they were screaming with amusement not horror. Children liked their freakshows. She gazed over the wall at the pyre, to focus on something while she figured out what to do.

Poor Raimi. Why had they picked up her man-child? She could not think of a reason. He really was nobody. As for herself, the Specials might assume she had died in the car. For all that had been, for all that was to come, Krista wished that she had. She knew now that the Banned-Film Club, her idea, her folly, must have put Raimi on an index. George Bailey and E.T. and Rick Deckard and all the rest, had colluded in betraying him. The authorities, she expected, were even now raiding the bar and her apartment and Sylvia's place, and Purgatory Films. Damo might be under arrest by now as well. And as for that son-of-a-bitch Bellingham –

Raimi was in the hands of God. All Krista could do was pray for him.

Oh but now it was too much. The weight of the air, carrying the barbecue stench of the driver's crackling flesh – even the weight of the air was too great for her now. She let it push her down, she consented to gravity and lay on the grass, submissive to whatever came next, her arms spread like the wings of an angel. Molecules each the mass of the sun, rested on her body. Krista expected never to rise again.

Episode VIII

The bruises on his arms were yellow now. He was a Raimi daiquiri. Early on, the cops had twisted each of his limbs. They had kicked him in the back too, leaving him with a dull pain in his spine. Someone had been about to stub a cigarette out on his forehead but the Superior had intervened and allowed only a few small slits with a box-cutter instead. Soon after that, they began to inject him with sedatives.

His cuts, scabbed over, stung. The sharp light hurt his eyes. He had been held in a cell in Rathmines but was now somewhere else. He did not know how much time had passed since his arrest. It was common practice, he had been told, to anaesthetise prisoners before moving, releasing or executing them. There was nothing in the rules about the use of anaesthetic during torture.

Here there was one white door and no windows. The walls enclosed a whitewashed hell, an invisible cage for the snowblind. By the door a deep white shelf protruded. On this sat an old terminal and a box of Marlboros but no lighter. Raimi had come to understand that the conditions in which he was being kept were not usual. Run-of-the-mill prisoners were held in communal blocks not much different from any other jail. But he was political, they had told him. This was a Blasphemy Division detention centre. Until then he had never heard of the Blasphemy Division.

Raimi made out shapes. Across from him sat two Detective Inquisitors. Mills, the one who appeared to want to procure Raimi's confession gently, was the only one in the room allowed to light cigarettes. The other one, Parker, did not have lighter privileges but asked for a smoke. Mills lit a cigarette and gave it to her. Why they both could not just do what they liked, Raimi didn't understand. There must be rules he hadn't been told about.

Soon Parker was tipping her cigarette into the ashtray on the table. She seemed wound up; she might strike at any moment. Raimi was more afraid of her than he was of Mills, because she had been so nice at the start. In his mind, he played her voice – an accumulation of memories, a remix video of Parker's greatest hits.

'I want to help you, Raimi. I want this to go smooth, so we can all get out of here. Remember, this is no fun for me, either, Raimi. You're innocent, right, but it's our job to see how innocent you are. We don't like. Do you think we like it when someone. When someone turns out to be. We don't. Raimi. Raimi, are you listening to me? I'm trying to be your friend here'.

Already today – had it been today? – Parker had got him to confess to the possession of illegal discs containing blasphemous material. Mills must have been jealous or perhaps it did not matter who got him to confess. Throughout all of this, the dialogue playing in his head, Parker's lips did not move. Could she be telepathic? It was possible.

'The Banned-Film Club indeed'. Here again was Parker's voice but in the present moment. She finished her cigarette and flicked the butt at him.

Mills got up, walked around the table and put a hand on the prisoner's head. Raimi's shoulders hurt. His brain hurt. His toenails hurt.

What had they done to his toenails?

'Let's start again'. Mills took his hand away. Raimi craned his neck to look at him as the D.I. leaned back against the wall. 'You've already told us you and Krista were never married'.

'What's wrong with that?'

'Not to each other'.

'Are you married?' Raimi's throat went dry. 'May I please have a smoke?'

'Sure, you may', Mills said, too affably. He got the cigarettes. He gave a Marlboro to Raimi, who put it in his mouth. Mills lit it. 'If you'd said "can I please have a smoke?" you wouldn't have got one'.

Raimi dragged on his cigarette and reflected that before coming to this room, he had only ever smoked joints. 'So all along I thought I was being pulled in for an act of public indecency and you say you're doing me for living in sin'.

'Pissing on the sperm bank'. Parker said.

'The Seminary', Raimi corrected her. He sucked on his smoke again.

'Whatever', Parker said. 'Defacing Jesus. That's a Class "A" Blasphemy right there. You shouldn't have hit the Transgression Booth either'.

'You're so trivial', Raimi said. 'You're so tiny. That isn't even his face'.

Though Raimi expected her to, Parker didn't smirk. 'We've had our eye on you for a while', she said. 'There are people in the Department a bit miffed at the way your whore served illegals in her bar. That's one thing. Physical blasphemy, or Class "A" defilement of our Lord and Saviour's image. That's another. Allowing banned material to be disseminated, that's another still. Quite the rap sheet'.

'Who was it?' Raimi heard his own weary voice and didn't trust it.

'Who do you think?' Mills spoke this time. His voice after so much of Parker's sounded out of place.

'What do you want from me?'

'Name the other members of the Banned-Film Club', Parker said.

'The Banned-Film Club?'

'Arrogant, calling it that', Parker said. 'Down with that sort of thing, I say'.

'What do you mean, *members* of the Banned-Film Club?'

'Who your contacts were. Who ran you'.

'I have no idea what you're on about'.

Mills took up the thread. 'We know there were others involved in this illegal organisation, this, if you will, unlawful assembly of insurgents'.

'You have to be putting me on'.

'Do you remember saying you were in the Blackrock chapter of the Anglican Militia?' Parker asked.

'Did I say that?' Raimi dropped his cigarette into the ashtray.

Parker pressed a button on the recorder set into the table. First came room static, then Raimi's drunken voice.

'... the Blackrock chapter of the Anglican Militia ...'

Parker paused the recording.

'Jesus!'

'Do you remember saying this too?' she asked, and pressed the button.

Raimi's voice again. 'Shit, we might as well bomb the Seminary'.

'We have to take these things seriously', Mills said.

'Why didn't you bring me in earlier, if you wanted me for all this stuff?'

'We were going to', Parker said.

'But some cop spotted me first'.

'That wasn't one of ours'. Mills said. 'That was some halfwit. Some *liudrámán*. We were about to pull that photo. But now you're here …'

'Now that you are here', Parker said, 'let's get right down to brass monkeys. Tell us what you were up to, there's a good little anarchist'.

'I want a lawyer'.

'You already have a lawyer', Mills said. 'You'll meet him when it's time'.

'I don't know anything about anything'.

'Our contact says you do. You very do indeed. He infiltrated your Banned-Film Club'. Parker snorted.

'Which name in itself gives something away', Mills added.

'If I was a terrorist, or whatever it is you think I am, would I pull your chain by calling my group something like that? Besides, who even knew about it?'

'You know who knew about it'.

'Exactly. Apart from me, there was only one member of the Banned-Film Club. Your guy'.

Mills burped. 'I think we'll come back tomorrow. Today, you're getting a cell of your own. Congratulations'.

Parker rapped on the door. A C-Special opened it and she whispered something to him. Two others entered. One handcuffed himself to Raimi.

'We made progress today', Mills said. He sounded faux-cheerful, like an actor on a one-take soap. 'Get some rest and we'll see you tomorrow, all right?'

He and Parker walked out.

The Specials waited a moment before taking him to a small, blank holding cell in which there was only a bed, a basin, a bucket and a bible. Someone had left a nude pinup of Madonna on the wall, but her breasts and genitals had been torn out.

The days went like this. Raimi was woken before dawn by the officer on duty banging a baton on the door. After his breakfast of toast, water and sedatives, the cops took him to the interrogation room. Either Parker or Mills came in first; they never arrived together. Sometimes one of them was hungover. They usually reeked of cigarette smoke. Whoever arrived first, inserted a new disk into the recording device and began asking questions. When the day's session was over, they always left together. After these two had started on the case, the ordinary cops had butted out and there were no more beatings or torture with blades, though the threat remained.

They had been grilling him for weeks now, going over old ground many times. He would tell them that he and Krista were not married and they would want to hear it again. He once let it slip that his colleague Bellingham reckoned he should find another job if editing propaganda films had become too much. They wanted to know what that meant, whether Bellingham was politically sound, and why he, Raimi, had a problem with such material when he had once worked on a commercial for an oil company. Then they asked him to tell them again. Other times, they came into the room and offered him a cigarette, which he took in anticipation of more questions, but they said nothing all morning. They sat there, not even looking at each other. He did not know what to make of that. Every so often, Parker left the room on the pretext of going to the 'little girl's room' and in her absence, Mills told him something about her, such as that she was just waiting for an excuse to open Raimi with a corkscrew, or gouge his eyes out with her dildo. It became clear that Mills was here to protect Raimi from the psychotic Parker. One time Mills went out to check his car. While he was gone Parker told Raimi that this hard-ass bastard she had to work with broke noses for sport.

Parker scrutinised Raimi but he did not meet her eyes. Taking lighter privileges that were not hers she lit a cigarette and puffed away on it, all the while watching him. She said nothing. Raimi had forgotten most of what he had told them already.

Mills came in with a box file. He put it on the table and began to pace the room very slowly, marching in an honour guard of one. Raimi was relieved to see him. He couldn't take any more of Parker's staring.

'Ok', Mills began. 'Now, I'm going to ask you a series of questions. Yes or no answers. Understood?'

'Yes …'

Mills lit a cigarette. 'We asked about you and Krista and we got sidetracked. Is she political? Yes or no'.

'No'.

'She wasn't the one who got those banned films for you'.

'No. That was Bellingham'.

'And you knew she was married when you got involved with her'.

'Yes'.

'And you admit to flouting the blasphemy laws by urinating on the face of Christ'.

'What? That wasn't his face! I told you. It's thirteenth century!'

'Yes or no'.

'Yes'.

'And you operated the Blackrock chapter of the Anglican Militia'.

'No'.

'You ran a covert group known as The Banned-Film Club'.

'It was not a covert group. We had a licence'.

Mills sat down. 'And you would like a cigarette'.

'Yes'. Raimi began to sob quietly.

Parker rolled her eyes. Mills didn't get up. He opened the box file, which was empty, then looked in it and shrugged at the prisoner.

'Sorry, bud. We're all out of smokes'.

The morning bell in the Unit rang at seven o'clock. Raimi was already awake and standing in front of the mirror when the officer banged on the door. As he splashed water on his face, Raimi saw that his beard had grown. This was a surprise to him. It was always a surprise.

Raimi's clothes were grubby now. He knew that he didn't deserve to have them clean. Outside his cell, the Specials were changing shifts. He heard yelling. A fight. The din of it began to stir his recurring headache. TV screens buzzed in the distance, voices mingling like atonal music in a wind tunnel. Footsteps. Night sticks on cell doors. A prisoner cried loudly in the next cell. Someone was being beaten up.

What would Mills and Parker have for him today? As he sat down on his bed, the door opened. Two Specials stood in the frame, blocking the way out. One of them said, 'You. Gerrup now, so'.

He rose and presented his right arm. The Special cuffed Raimi to himself.

'Do I get any breakfast?'

'Don't be smart, you'.

Raimi decided not to argue. They took him down the corridor to the white room. The other Special opened the door and the one handcuffed to Raimi led them in. He released his prisoner and pushed him into the room. The two Specials left, locking the door behind them.

Raimi didn't sit down at once. He went to the shelf to look for cigarettes. He found the packet already open with the lighter beside it, so he lit a Marlboro and inhaled. He considered the facts. They had got him to agree to everything. They had twisted his ordinary life into a campaign of insubordination, illegality and terrorism. With his diet of drugs, he had forgotten himself. Raimi was just some guy, some fellow he barely remembered, from somewhere he'd hardly ever been.

Krista had not tried to get in touch. Nobody had come to his assistance. He was disappointed in everybody.

After his second cigarette, Raimi sat in the chair to wait. Parker came in. She stood looking down at him but said nothing. Mills arrived shortly after that, along with a tall man in a suit, who carried a briefcase that he placed on the table.

'Are you my lawyer?'

'Aeneas Dunsmore', the man said. 'At your service'.

There weren't enough chairs, so Mills let Parker and the lawyer sit.

'Anus Dinsmore'.

'Dunsmore'.

'Where were you when I needed you?'

'You need me now', the lawyer said.

'They'll be bringing your breakfast in soon', Mills said. He hovered by the door.

Parker leaned back in her chair to let the lawyer take over.

'Now, Raimi', Dunsmore said, 'there are certain matters we must attend to'.

He opened his briefcase and took out a form, which he pushed across to Raimi. From his breast pocket he lifted a very fine pen.

'What's that? A confession?'

'It's your statement'.

'I haven't made any statement'.

'Not that kind of statement. Account payable'.

'What?'

Dunsmore passed him the pen. 'This confirms that you waive legal costs and that your next-of-kin agrees to refund the outgoings of the State in …'

Raimi signed the paper without reading it. 'Is that it?'

'That's it', the lawyer said. He replaced the paper in his briefcase. He nodded at the pen in Raimi's hand and when the other man failed to give it back, Dunsmore snatched it and put that in his briefcase too. The lawyer cleared his throat. 'Now, Raimi, I'll be representing you. I will make a written deposition on your behalf'.

'Which means?'

Parker caught Mills's look of disbelief and returned it with interest.

Dunsmore sounded flustered. 'It means that you present your case in an appropriate manner'.

There came a knock at the door. Mills answered it. A C-Special entered, pushing a breakfast trolley. It held a plate of bacon and eggs, a pile of toast and two large pots, one containing coffee, the other tea. What was this, a hotel? The cop set the table and poured tea with too much ceremony for the occasion; then he left without looking back.

'Enjoy your breakfast, Raimi', Mills said. 'This one's on the house'.

Episode IX

Krista's ribs hurt and she was sure there was a bruise on her face. She felt a tender spot in her left cheek. Her legs were weak but she walked on. One of the bars she passed on her way to Kennedy's, was called Reactor Number Four. Another was named The Geiger Counter. The old shopping centre was now an apartment block housing over five hundred families. The former bowling alley had been consecrated as the local Orthodox Church. There didn't seem to be any shops here that were just shops. Mostly, Krista knew, commerce in Chernobyltown happened in the bars, and was usually black market. Alcohol was distributed through the regular channels but other supplies could be had if you knew the right people. Czech absinthe, old French paperbacks, Lebanese red, Irish vegetables ... If you wanted something special, you had to be in the know. This made for a close-knit community though Chernobyltown was not small. It covered an area that used to encompass the old boroughs of Phibsboro and Drumcondra. Twenty years before, descendants of the disaster had begun to arrive, eventually creating an enclave and adopting English – this amused some – as their *lingua franca*.

The locals blended their native culture with ironic references to nuclear power. Where there used to be an Italian chipper, now stood an Atomic Grill. There was also the Strontium Kennel, a nightclub designed after a large nuclear fallout shelter; here physically disabled people were hired as waiters. In the Kennel, nuclear-themed movies played in a continuous loop. Films such as *Threads, The War Game, The Bed Sitting Room* and *The Day After* ran in rotation.

Damo had told her that his contact's I.D. chips were made so well that they would fool any official, any machine. She could get herself identified as an Illegal, and deported to some detention centre in France or Spain. She would find it hard at first but the authorities in whatever country she ended up in, would let her go after a while and she could begin a new life. Krista felt a twinge in her right shoulder and wondered where her chip would be implanted. She was determined that her identity would never disappear – she would always be Krista.

On Cesium Boulevard, she began to notice the people. Once themselves refugees, they were ordinary Dubliners now. Mothers wheeled children in electric prams. Bigger kids ran in the traffic. A businessman in a sharp suit crossed at the lights. An old woman in a plastic raincoat, haggled with a vendor at a stall selling TV pads. Two workers, wearing overalls with utility belts that held guns as well as laser cutters, passed her in the street. Krista didn't see any C-Specials; the police tended to leave Chernobyltown alone. It was said that the government ran the lion's share of the dealing that went on here but Krista was not so sure. An urban myth had it that somewhere, in the bowels of a tenement, a stock of wild plutonium had gone underground, liberated from the disintegrating Ukrainian nuclear programme and brought to Ireland in a suitcase, on a boat. That was surely not true, or someone would have used it already.

By now her mother would have been cremated. Krista tried not to think about that.

It was getting on for five when she made it to the end of Cesium. Kennedy's was near. Krista knew its ancient notoriety as the place in which a Taoiseach used to drink, pretending to be one of the people. She had been in this pub herself a few times in her youth and remembered it as a pleasant watering hole.

Before she took the corner she heard a commotion, and as she turned she saw a stolen APC on fire in the middle of the street. There were no personnel on board. Children threw stones at the vehicle as it blazed then they ran back and returned with more stones. That was a good sign. It meant that she would likely find a sympathetic reception in Kennedy's. Ratko was the guy's name, Damo had said, but who the hell was called Ratko these days? That didn't matter. He was one of the people around here with whom the police definitely did not fuck, though that might not be saying much.

Krista hurried past the kids with their bonfire, and darted in the front door of the pub. This bar was a throwback. It had no TV, no internet. It was many a decade, she knew, since the internet had been secure. No one used it for anything secret. There was a strange hum in the place as though all the fridge doors were open. At this hour, the workers from the mill up the road had finished their shift. Some were gathered at a big table down the back. A journalist or two, on the trail of a hot story, might be found elsewhere in the bar, but Krista would not recognise them. The barman, whose tag identified him as Boris – probably not his birth name – was pulling a pint of Guinness for a customer. Krista approached and waited. The customer took his pint and walked away.

'What can I get you?' Boris asked.

'I'm looking for Ratko'.

'One moment'. Boris punched a communicator button by the spirits cabinet and buzzed the back office. 'Someone here to see you'.

'Who is it?' came a voice on the speaker. Ratko had a Finglas accent.

'One moment'. Boris looked over at Krista. 'Who is it?'

'Krista Wallace. Damo sent me'.

'Krista Wallace. Damo sent her'.

'Take her through'.

Boris stepped out from behind the bar then led her into a musty corridor at the end of which was Ratko's office. This place smelled of damp and rats. The barman opened the door and held it for her. She walked through and he left her to her meeting.

'Krista', said Ratko. 'Krista Wallace. Sit down. Damo told me you were coming. He told me what happened. Shocking'.

'How the hell did he know that? It only happened today'.

'Word gets around'.

Ratko was a thin man, looking not at all as she had expected him to. He was in his early thirties but by the lines on his face, and his baldness, he seemed older, with a scar that ran all the way down his left cheek and into his big grey moustache. He sat behind a large oak desk covered in papers and roll-up computer fabrics. A foot-tall pewter model of a Xenomorph stood on the left-hand corner of this desk. There were no windows in the room, which was lit unevenly by a lamp on the floor and a flickering fluorescent panel overhead.

Krista sat at the desk. 'I believe you can organise some papers. A chip'.

Ratko sized her up. 'Papers. A chip'.

'I want a new I.D. Someone who'll be deported with no questions asked. If you're not trying to leave, they won't stop you'.

'Nice logic', he said, 'but I'm a businessman. Businessmen have their own brand of logic'.

Krista reached inside her handbag to get the brown envelope full of cash. As she did, Ratko put a hand under his desk. Krista stopped moving. 'You don't need that'. She gave him a look of steel. 'I'm here to do business too'.

'You never can tell', he said and relaxed back into his seat.

Krista brought the envelope out and put it on the desk. 'My collateral'.

Ratko looked at her with distrust. 'I do not want your money'.

'Why not?'

'I can make things easier for you. I can get you a proper I.D. of a respectable alien who has a *right* to come and go as she pleases. None of this deportee shit for you, Krista Wallace'. Ratko stared her out. 'In return there is something you will do for me'.

Krista sat up straight. 'What are we talking about here?'

'You are in trouble', Ratko said, 'or you would not have come to me'.

'Yes'.

'Good. And you want to get away. Very sensible, very clever'.

Krista was not sure just how sensible or clever she was.

Ratko noted her unease. 'Now this is what you will do for me'.

'I'm listening'. Krista retrieved the envelope and replaced it in her bag.

'You will take some merchandise to a customer of mine', Ratko said. 'A government man'.

'How do I know you're not setting me up?'

'I could hand you over right now if I wanted to. You would be raped in jail before they killed you. But you are useful. Listen now. This man gets certain items from me. He runs a small business and I know he samples the stuff. He pays in cash but occasionally he is amenable to a little barter. In this case, I will ask him to make you disappear. Poof. You will take a package from me to him and in return you get an implant that fools the retina scanners at the airport and shows up a fake I.D. on their system. But you will not be a mere Illegal. You get to travel first class as a proper citizen with a proper identity in London'.

'That's impressive. If your chip is so good, why do you need your government man?' Krista shifted in her seat.

'I do not need him. You do. I said this is the man who can make you disappear. The chip is only part of it. You also need someone amenable on the official end of things. This man can have every record of you expunged and replaced. He can lose you completely and find you again as someone else'.

There was something disturbing about that thought. Krista wasn't sure if she wanted to disappear forever, to have nothing left of her, to walk away as a new person, even if that was a person of standing.

'I told Damo he could have the bar if he got me out'.

'Damo is my nephew'.

She hadn't seen that one coming. 'He told me he was called Damo O'Neill'.

'He is. Damo is short for Dimitri. Good Irish name'. Ratko shifted in his seat like he had suddenly felt a stab of piles.

'So that means you get the bar too'.

'Damo is my nephew'.

Krista sighed and it seemed to her like a betrayal of her vulnerability. She cursed herself.

'Now', Ratko said. 'There is another reason why you will do this for me. It is a personal reason and my own men must not be involved'.

'Personal?'

Ratko rapped the palm of his hand on the desk. 'Listen to me and I will tell you. This man has had relations with my daughter. That is not a good move unless you are my daughter's husband, and they are all dead'.

'You must have been upset that he did that to you'.

'Oh yes, I was very upset and as a man of honour I had to respond. I cut off not his tiny little penis, as I should have done, but his supply of merchandise. He is nervous now. I expect he is desperate. I expect now his customers are asking questions. So the plan is this. I will forgive him his little crime against nature and reinstate him as a client in exchange for his arranging your transformation'.

'I don't understand'.

Ratko sighed heavily. 'You bring him his regular supply, but the consignment is contaminated. I told you he samples his own shit and this is cut with something very slow and effective. He will not even feel sick for a while. He will not die for months. This is good. Knowing that he is dying, that is priceless like MasterCard. I like to savour my pleasures for as long as possible. You only live once. When I know he is close to death, when he knows it himself, then I will have him brought in and cut off his tiny little penis'.

'Elegant. And wrong'.

'You do not tell me what is wrong. When he has erased you, and you escape, then you tell me what is wrong'.

Krista tasted bile in her mouth. Slowly she gathered herself and knew that this was her only way out. It didn't matter about the bar.

She looked Ratko in the eye. 'We have a deal'.

The cold bastard made a tent of his hands. 'Good', he said. 'But Krista Wallace, how do I know you will keep your side of our arrangement?'

Krista tilted her head slightly to indicate her acceptance. 'You don't. But I will'.

'Excellent', Ratko said. 'Now join me for a drink'.

Ratko stood at the bar while Krista, exhausted, sat. She thought of poor Raimi and could not imagine where he was right now, or what was being done to him. Ratko was entirely the opposite of her lover. She did not know whether to think of him as a crime boss or as a civic leader. He was the devil with whom she must deal; she understood that. Now she tasted a metal tang in her mouth and felt a chill in her stomach. She might be coming down with something worse than regret.

'Boris, two Scotches', Ratko said.

Boris poured from a very old bottle with a deferential flourish that Krista thought satirical. He set the drinks in front of them. This scotch was the best in the house, no doubt. For a moment she concentrated on that: the anticipation of its sting.

The buzz she had heard before in this room had gone now. There were voices still, but they were muted. Did everyone whisper when the Boss was around?

Ratko sipped his whisky while Krista considered hers. The thin man made no secret of glancing at her breasts. He took his time with them before looking away to the bottles behind the bar. Boris smiled coldly at her.

Ratko turned back to catch her gaze. 'You could stay here, you know. I would protect you. We could make a good team'.

'You were checking out my breasts', Krista said. 'What kind of team did you have in mind?'

'You may have what it takes'. Ratko said. 'See how tomorrow goes and let's think about it, yes?'

Krista downed her drink in one and set the glass upside-down on the bar. She made a whisky face.

Ratko laughed at this. 'You will stay here tonight. No one will touch you, I promise. Tomorrow you make the delivery. I will arrange your driver'.

'Not Damo'.

'No'.

Ratko's expression contained a core of pity wrapped in indifference. It was a curious thing, Krista saw, a glimmer of humanity frozen in him. But what was a human other than a vicious excuse for a monkey?

'I must go now'. Ratko turned to leave.

Krista put her hand on his arm. 'The kids outside were burning an APC', she said. 'I don't think it'll be long before the Specials tear this place down'.

Ratko paused. 'You've heard about the plutonium. They think we can use it to make a bomb, that we'd nuke Dublin if they tried to take over'.

'Jesus. And would you?'

'A suitcase can be left anywhere'.

Episode X

The clock over the bench said fifteen past Elvis. Raimi didn't see the number but that's what he told himself was there. Sunlight streamed in through the window overhead, too high for anyone to climb out. Sedated, he sat chained to a C-Special. Beside them both, Dunsmore busied himself with papers.

The voice boomed out across the room. 'Call 11.339B.3X. Approach the bench'.

A C-Special pushed a small man in prison cottons forward. The man was bald and gaunt. He seemed not to notice as the Sentencing Officer pronounced: 'You have been found guilty of the creation and distribution of pornographic material'.

The man didn't react.

'Under God and the State, I sentence you to deocularisation, to be carried out immediately'.

The prisoner began to cry spontaneously, making the most of his eyes while he could. His C-Special took him away through a grey door. The man would now be sent to an Absolution Room, where sentence would be carried out, followed by medical assistance to prevent his death from loss of blood. Raimi thought of the Invisible Man in reverse.

You never knew when your number would be called. There was no apparent system, so Raimi waited, blankly. Sedatives fogged his mind. He thought the C-Special was his stupidly dressed twin.

Raimi felt no hatred for any of them: the Sentencing Officer, this policeman, the useless lawyer. He didn't think about Bellingham and he didn't remember Krista except as a face in a daydream that momentarily broke through the fog.

'14.459C.3Y. Car theft. You are sentenced to five years behind a wheel'.

'13.329F.3O. Trafficking in heretical objects. You are sentenced to stigmata'.

The day wore on.

'145.554S.3H ... Please approach the something ... something ... acts of terrorism and conspiracy to cause ... something. C&D ... carried out by something ... may God have mercy on your ... something'.

Raimi was walking now, ahead of the C-Special to whom he was chained. The lawyer did not accompany them.

Someone said C&D.

Raimi thought it was a funny way to describe what was not funny at all. It sounded like a brand of petfood. Cookies & Dalmations. Cheese & Dust. Clitoris & Dostoevsky. He wondered who the lucky sod was then realised it was him. He was already standing at the bench, still attached to the cop. The Sentencing Officer was saying these things to him, to Raimi. By the time he was led away he had forgotten whatever that guy had gone on about. He was thinking of a news item from years ago: 'The bodies of

96 Egyptian passengers who died in the crash of Gulf Air Flight Blah Blah were flown home today …' Raimi thought that surely after such a disaster they'd think twice about getting on a plane again.

If there is no future there is nothing to fear. Raimi's consciousness resolved in a new white room that was not the interrogation chamber. He felt neither terror nor panic. He only knew that his thoughts were a lie. Raimi lied now in his thoughts. There was a recorder hidden in the wall. Someone was listening to his breathing. Someone was counting those breaths. Their equipment could pick up his heartbeat: systole and diastole measuring the span of his life, but he knew the measurements were also a lie. He found this calibration interesting all the same. Fear and joy both take time away, speeding the call and response of the heartbeat but here he needed neither emotion. They had kept him on the drugs. According to Dunsmore, he had two weeks at most but what were two weeks when there was no time at all? The clock in this room had stopped at twelve. It had been both noon and midnight forever. The white room might be a screen, the film of his life projected on the walls, but who would pay to see that? He thought about all the strange things people did to their bodies. He considered the Chinese practice of footbinding and speculated that his own limbs might be bound like this before being removed. C&D. The art of tattoo: they slice the skin with a sharp blade and insert the dye. False-limb syndrome. Would he imagine himself to be whole? He had read about amputees who felt pain in limbs that were no longer there. Would it be the same for him? Would he have time to get used to his altered form? Then: Where is Krista? *What am I here for?* In many respects, he was already only half a person. He had forgotten the names of his parents. He did not remember why he and Krista had been together. 'Raimi' was something that had occurred to him, like a line from a song whispered by a dead choir. My name is Raimi. I am the text in the Book of Raimi. I will live in infamy as the man who urinated on Seminary Twelve. I will be remembered as a terrorist who conspired in the Banned-Film Club. I will be forgotten. In the end I will be unimportant, as will Bellingham Iscariot. There will be a headstone but no dates. This is a name without a life, without a time. But I will still have a name. He dismissed the thought: a name is nothing without DNA. DNA is an anagram of AND. Together they made a palindrome that sounds like the crying of a baby. Life goes on, its needs always fulfilled, the individual a host.

In his dreams, Raimi regressed to childhood. A single image recurred: himself as a boy in a playground, on a swing, jumping off. But he couldn't fly, and he banged his head, breaking it open so that he needed stitches. His mother stood behind him, laughing at his hubris, finding his ambition amusing. His innocent, optimistic leap off the swing seemed to stand for his whole life. He had always been ridiculed by those who were supposed to show him the way. And here it came again, the tarmacadam ground, ready to split his skull and air the brain, letting it fall out so that he might know a more refined sense of pain, with the whole planet as an instrument. I am five years old. Can you hear me? I am five. The years are peeling away. I am five, and I can ride a bike. Who was he now? The clock still said twelve. It didn't say Elvis. It didn't even say Johnny Cash. Raimi sat in a wheelchair, back in the white room. His arms were missing. A mirror stood in front of him, full length, so that he could contemplate his mutilated form. The wounds were raw and bandaged. He couldn't see his arms. Was this some kind of mistake? He could always go back for them.

I'm going mad.

Disembodied arms floated against the white of the wall before him.

I'm going.

He tried to reach out with his mind and claim a pair for himself, but his mind, needing arms to find a pair of arms, failed.

I'm.

He screamed but only a gagging husk of a sound emerged.

Breathe in zero atmosphere.

Tears.

Air unequal to the notes.

When the drugs wore off, he would be past screaming.

Two weeks. It would all be over in two weeks.

The time was permanently twelve.

Uniform with the whiteness of the surrounding walls, the invisible door said: out there is the same as in here. I'm in the mirror now. The man in the mirror is me. I'm the Invisible Man in reverse.

A tall man dressed in the uniform of the C-Specials, walked into the room. Raimi stared. When was the last time they had brought him food? How would he eat it now? The man had brought no food. He closed the door behind him and took a scroll from his left breast pocket. Why had they sent a person?

'Prisoner 145.554S.3H', the man said. He sounded dour. 'You have been found guilty of blasphemy and other sundry felonies, and have been sentenced to C&D, part of which sentence has been carried out in accordance with the procedures laid down in the terms of the Provisional Tribunal. The remainder of your sentence will be executed at 0800 hours tomorrow morning. A chaplain will be provided so that you may make your peace with God. You will receive your final meal in due course. That is all'.

The man turned on his heel, military style, and strode out of the room, slamming the door behind him.

That was weird.

Raimi began to listen to the clock, a tick, tick that he must have imagined, because the clock was not working. He drifted into sleep again, the pain in his stumps throbbing through the anaesthetic.

The ticking was there again when he woke. It was not coming from the wall, nor had he imagined it. It was coming from inside his head, just below the skin.

'They don't tell you about the bomb', the chaplain said. 'That's a little administrative thing. I must say I agree with their reason but not their method'.

Raimi had nothing to discuss with him regarding theological matters, but this was news.

The chaplain wore a C-Specials insignia over the left breast of his uniform-soutane. He looked older than his years, haggard and used, a slave to appetites that had drained his youth and the youths of others. He stood between Raimi and the mirror. There was nowhere for him to sit.

'There's a bomb?'

'It's in case you manage to get out, unlikely though that may be. You haven't noticed the stitches on the back of your head, I take it'.

Raimi couldn't reach behind his head to feel for the scar.

'It's been there for a while. Small yield. They implanted it shortly after your conviction'.

'What are you here for?'

'I was framed', the chaplain said with a serious face. 'I was set up'. Then his composure broke and he burst into laughter. 'Ha. No, I'm the chaplain'.

'You're an asshole. Now, what are you here for?'

'You might need spiritual comforting'.

'Do you have any food?'

'Now I'll ask you to let me say my piece, if you don't mind, without interruption'.

'Go ahead. I might as well fill my last few hours with asshole mumbo jumbo'.

'First I want to pray with you, ok? That's in the rules. I want you to go to your reward with an unblemished soul'.

'Christ on a cock'.

The chaplain groaned at this further blasphemy. What did one more matter now? With a certain kindness he bent down and whispered into Raimi's ear. 'I have news for you, my son. A message from Krista'.

Raimi resisted the urge to cry out with the bewilderment he felt inside him like an infection. Krista, who didn't come back for him.

The chaplain continued. 'She's safe. She's carrying your child, Raimi'.

When did that happen?

DNA is an anagram of AND.

Nature cares nothing about the individual.

On the other hand, 'oceanic' is an anagram of 'cocaine'.

You can make anything out of anything.

The chaplain stood up straight. 'If you'd like me to keep vigil with you, I'll arrange for a chair to be brought in. I think your soul is in pretty good shape, my son'.

'Thank you, Father', Raimi said, 'but I'm an atheist'.

'As you wish', the chaplain said. 'I'll tell them to bring in your meal'. Then he put out his hand to shake, and realised his mistake. 'Sorry'.

Raimi started to laugh then cry and the chaplain couldn't bring himself to leave. He put his arms around Raimi's head in an effort to comfort him, until the young man's tears had stopped. The chaplain stood back, made the sign of the cross and said, 'I will pray for you, even if you're an atheist. The Lord loves them too, apparently'.

'You'd better get out of here before I punch you in the mouth'.

'I won't insult you with platitudes', the chaplain said, 'but may I offer you the host?'

'Fuck off'.

From his inside pocket, the chaplain withdrew a silver box that looked like a cigarette case. He held it open. It was full of blessed wafers. He offered one to Raimi, who had neither the will nor the means to resist. Raimi opened his mouth wide and stuck out his tongue. Up yours, Jesus.

'Body of Christ'. The chaplain placed the host on Raimi's tongue. He closed the silver case and put it back inside his pocket. 'Don't spit that one out, Raimi. You'll see. It's a powerful thing, the host'. He made the sign of the cross and left the room, closing the door behind him.

It was years since Raimi had tasted this stuff but he remembered the flavour and wanted some ice cream to go with it. Allowing the wafer to melt on his tongue, Raimi hated himself for having let the chaplain force it on him.

Some time later he discovered an interesting new fact. The host, this host, was laced with the most powerful and wonderful LSD. He hoped for a good trip. Maybe David Gilmour would appear in person and play him something great.

After an indeterminate time, the butterflies in his stomach found themselves in outer space, wings unfolding gracefully to take the ion wind that would propel them gently beyond the moon, out of the solar system and on towards the farthest galaxies, gathering power like a Von Neumann machine of the soul.

With any luck, the LSD would see him through to the end and he would go out smiling, off his head on eternity itself.

Built for men without arms, three mechanical crucifixes lay flat on the ground. The crosses represented a modern version of an ancient device. Each accompanied by a pair of orderlies, two prisoners – mutilated, sedated – awaited the final act, slumped in their wheelchairs.

The chaplain and the governor stood near the entrance to the yard. The governor glanced up to the glass-walled room that overhung the yard. Inside sat a company of prison officers and three C-Specials from Rathmines. There was a delegation from Amnesty International, two nervous-looking Nigerian women. Elaine Brooks was not there. Neither was Damo. Nor was Bellingham. And where was Krista?

It was raining lightly. An orderly wheeled Raimi out as another man walked behind them. They stopped in front of the cross in the middle. Raimi looked around but couldn't make out much. He was having the most appalling comedown. The LSD had worn off. This he felt keenly, despite the other pharmaceuticals sloshing around in his veins. Reality was assaulting him just when he needed reality to sod off and leave him alone. Reality was enjoying a cruel laugh at his expense. Then again, reality was good at that sort of thing.

Now that everyone was here, the governor spoke.

After the preamble, Raimi listened in, overhearing his own fate.

'You have been found guilty of capital offences against the State and God and sentenced to termination by means of C&D. It is my solemn duty therefore to direct that the remainder of your sentences be executed immediately. May God have mercy on your immortal souls'.

He finished with something in Irish, some martyr's prayer. For all that Raimi knew or cared it might have been a shopping list, or one of the poems that Padraig Pearse had written in praise of much younger men.

When the governor had said his piece, the orderlies took their charges and placed them flat on the crucifixes before securing each of them with one strap across the chest, one across the ankles. Then all six orderlies stood back.

'The chaplain will now give the final prayer', the governor said.

Raimi didn't see the chaplain but it was the man who had visited him. Reverted into an official again, the holy man held a psalter and read from a sheet placed in it like a bookmark.

'It is by the power invested in me by the Lord God that I bid you peace and farewell as you embark on the final journey across the threshold into eternal life, taking with you only your souls. May you awake in the glory and joy of the Lord God, Jesus Christ himself, who sits at the right hand of the Father for ever and ever. Amen'.

Raimi tried to wriggle and found that he could not.

The governor mumbled something. Then he nodded to one of the prison guards, who pressed a button on the wall.

Thus activated, the crucifixes began to protest against gravity – a force of nature challenged now by the works of Man. Raimi sensed the horizon shifting as the butterflies in his stomach dropped dead, their wings in flames. The crosses rose slowly and the skin of the world peeled away and the sky came down to receive these three lost souls. Gravity fought back and dragged on him but the power of the cross was too strong. Their crucifixes rose slowly to the vertical, forming a mournful tableau in the image of three Thalidomide Christs.

Episode XI

D.I. Bellingham and his wife Maura sat in a pew. As usual, Church 34 at Phibsboro Nexus was full. It had been a very fruitful mass. A middle-aged man had admitted to beating his wife and been led away by stern Priests. A young woman had given herself up as a fornicator but had refused to name her accomplice. There had even been a cure: a crippled boy, whose legs had never worked, had risen from his wheelchair, shuffled out in front of the congregation and declared himself a future triathlete. Pater Joseph had then delivered a powerful sermon about alcohol abuse.

Now the crowd dispersed into the sheeting rain. Bellingham was thankful for his long leather coat. Maura had on an ankle-length cotton dress, imprinted with the images of blue fish. If they didn't get to the car soon she would come to resemble an aquarium, Bellingham thought but did not dare to say. She was in her sixties now, with wiry hair, still blonde, and a Glass clamped over her left eye. He thought of her as his rock. This formidable woman had just retired as General Secretary of the Gene Pool. Even though her team had failed so far to discover the gene for sanctity, her reputation was unimpeachable. Her husband respected her always and without question although he did not now think to offer her his coat.

Bellingham and his wife crossed to the Ford Tarsus parked outside the betting shop. That establishment, he knew, was a front for the secret brothel habitually attended by members of the Oireachtas. Such men and women as worked there were known colloquially as 'Dáil Privileges'. As they sat into the vehicle, Bellingham wondered if the Thalidomide Taoiseach himself ever visited the knocking shop. These days no one speculated publicly about either his morals or his age.

They set out on the road to Glasnevin. It was a good day to watch the interments. Bellingham turned to Maura. Before he could say anything she pursed her lips. 'Keep your eye on the road'.

'Right, love'.

At the cemetery Bellingham parked. Maura got out first and stretched her legs. He followed her in. There were five funerals scheduled for today and they couldn't go to them all so they chose to attend the burial of an omnisexual dealer in absinthe who gloried in the name Sebastian Melmoth. At his trial he had remarked that if they could, the authorities would arrest the trees in autumn for littering.

It was a good, long ceremony and the rain subsided for the duration. Pater O'Toole delivered a little talk about denial of self. Then, the coffin lowered, the grave covered over, people began to leave. On the way out, Maura noticed a headstone.

'That one'.

'What?'

'Stop', Maura said, and she adjusted her Glass. 'Raimi O'Connor'.

Bellingham stopped. The name sounded familiar.

'That headstone'. Maura pointed to Raimi's grave.

Bellingham was quiet for a moment as he bowed his head, but not in prayer. He squinted to read the inscription on the headstone. *Raimi O'Connor – Blasphemer, Adulterer, Terrorist.* There were no dates. The Lost didn't get dates.

'One day', Bellingham said, 'he'll be forgotten like all the others'.

'Wasn't he one of yours?'

'Him?' Bellingham said, 'No. I just knew him. They nailed Raimi O'Connor long before I got into this game. I worked with him once. He was a nice young man. Some Ukrainian turned him in'.

Maura pursed her lips. She squeezed Bellingham's hand and they turned away. 'I could have sworn he was your first', she said.

As they got into the car, he hardly noticed that the rain had resumed. Starting the engine, Bellingham thought about Raimi then shook his head. 'All he wanted to do was watch some films. Someone in the Department needed an example. An early test case'.

'How would you know that, if it wasn't you?'

'It was eight years ago. How am I supposed to remember?'

A happy thought came to him then, a better thought. He and Maura were invited to come over next Thursday to Pater Thomas's compound in Foxrock. It would be just the three of them. Jo, the Pater's House Companion, had been seconded to the Legion on a long-term mission in Angola. Pater Thomas had promised dinner followed by a showing of *The Exorcist,* a film he considered a most effective warning against the occult and which therefore could be watched with impunity despite its status. The Paters enjoyed certain perks, certain dispensations. Bellingham liked to benefit from that occasionally. He knew that when you found a good Pater, you kept in with him.

'Captain Howdy, Lamb of God', he said. 'Pazuzu, Defender of the Faith'.

'What in the name of Jesus are you on about?'

Bellingham shrugged and put his foot down but only to shorten the journey.

Entering Griffith Avenue he had to slow the car again. There was a roadblock ahead. It was no wonder. Only last week, the Militia had bombed the Concert Hall.

Three Priests attended this roadblock. These ones looked freshly hatched, only a few months out of the Seminary. One waved down the Ford Tarsus and raised his machine gun.

Bellingham slowed the car and rolled the window open as the Priest approached. 'May I help you, Father?'

The Priest, a towering clone in a bulletproof combat soutane and a black metal helmet, kept his machine gun raised. These guys, Bellingham knew, stood exactly six foot tall in their bare feet. They had poise and their kick could kill you.

'Reginald Bellingham?' The clone darted a glance at his wristphone. His voice had no discernible accent.

'Looking for a group of rogue cellists, Father? Haven't seen them'.

'Could you please alight from your vehicle, sir'.

'Beg pardon?'

'Out of the car, please, sir'. The Priest sounded too polite. His two clone-brothers, on the other side of the car now, peered in at the back seat. They raised their own weapons.

'Do you know who I *am*?'

'Yes, sir, I do', the Priest replied. 'That is the point. New regulations. You are now an illegal foreigner'.

Maura tutted and stared out. The Priest on her side of the car tapped his gun against the glass. She jumped back.

'Jesus'. Bellingham obeyed the Priest and got out of the car. If they were now rounding up Yorkshiremen, what had the world come to? He turned to the clone, who put a hand on his arm.

'Come with me'.

'So I'm a foreigner now. I see', Bellingham said. He shook his head then let himself be led away. 'And tell me this, you bloody Priest. What country are you from?'

Episode XII

Raimi awoke already in motion. A bright blue sky slipped past overhead. Unable to rise, he felt a snake of pain coil around his guts, an anti-anaesthetic anaconda pinning him down. He sensed the wires and tubes attached to his body, attempting to turn him into a Christmas tree. He wanted to scream but the mask over his mouth and nose prevented it. He heard no breathing, not even his own.

Then came a submarine *bip*. It reminded him of sonar. He had heard it before. Now he heard it again. Bip. Bip. Bip.

In the silences between the notes, came voices, panicked all around him in a collage of franticity. Lights flickered just at the edge of his vison. Something crackled in his head but it could have been his skull turning to dust.

Gas sighed through him and he faded, grateful for the mist and the blackness it parted to reveal. Before he fell into the dark, Raimi heard another, solitary voice. It was that of a woman, sharp and bitter, resigned after hours of defeat and no rest.

'*Merde*'.

Her voice red-shifted away.

The last *bip* went on with no gaps. It transformed into a needle of sound that filled Raimi's head and expanded into a field. The sound became light. He had seen it before.

Episode XIII

From the top of the Eiffel Tower, Krista could see the whole of Paris, or what she thought to be the whole of Paris. She flicked a glance up at the remains of the dead telecommunications equipment above the observation deck. Down below, she had already peered in at the private apartment in which Gustave Eiffel had entertained guests. It was home to the waxworks mannequins of Eiffel, his daughter and Thomas Edison. The apartment commemorated a visit by the American scientist to Paris in 1889. A girder split the room and reminded occupants of where they were, and of how unusual it was that anyone should so casually take his *café au lait* and croissants this high up.

Wrapped in a long black coat, her hair naturally grey now like her mother's, Krista cast a burnt-out figure on the dark metal tower. She thought the ruins above bestowed a sense of completion. Only when something had started to be destroyed, was the building of it definitively over. She liked that the entire tower had been constructed to move in the wind, to bend rather than break. If she stood here for long enough she would feel the sway and it would enter her bones, it would make her a reed.

It was late afternoon. Louisa, her six-year-old daughter, was out there in the city, sitting in a warm classroom.

Krista took a deep breath. The winter air chilled the tourists below but up here it was icy. She shivered to touch the new wire mesh on the observation deck; this had been installed to deter potential Eiffel-jumpers, of which there had recently been a spate. *Le Monde* speculated as to where these men got the money for tickets if they were so destitute; and why they didn't spend it on a meal, or on wine.

Despite the swelling of tourists continually feeding from the queues at the base of the Tower up the narrow staircases to the lifts; despite the crush of visitors all around her, Krista felt alone.

Amiel was at work now, cutting the negative of the sixty-eighth official Woody Allen film. Once a year, in memory of the Manhattanite, a new picture was made by The Fall Project, a foundation of Parisian Allen aficionados, and credited to him as director. This movie, *Anhedonia,* would be the late Allen's final film. It had been shot on 35mm film. The UGC Danton was now planning the first-ever season of his complete *oeuvre,* including this last posthumous work. Just because you were dead it didn't mean you couldn't still create. That was a French attitude of which Krista approved. They had found a print of *Men of Crisis: The Harvey Wallinger Story* and would be showing that as well. Krista didn't care for Woody Allen's films but did like his *Standup Comic* record, to which Amiel had introduced her. If she closed her eyes while listening to it, she might as well be back in a nightclub in 1964, enjoying a candlelit dinner with some suave Dean Martin lookalike in a tuxedo, while the ginger funnyman bashfully undersold his astonishing sexual prowess.

Eight years gone, Krista reflected. Raimi was dust now, assumed into the currents of the multiverse, transmuted into a purer form. Dust was honest. Dust was the purest thing going.

When Amiel had met her at Heathrow all those years ago, they took the tube together into London and resumed their marriage more or less from where they had left off. It was, he said, their reverse divorce. Krista didn't respond to his warmth at first. She was surprised by it, caught short by the fact of it. Why would he be warm towards her? That assumption at least, was like old times.

Months later they moved to Paris and almost as soon as they arrived, Amiel found a job. None of this had mattered at the time. It took Krista months to begin to feel normal with him but Amiel was patient. Even now, she saw a shrink twice a week, a former Jesuit who had found Freud and converted.

She eventually rediscovered her affection for her old husband. Her miscarriage, that inexplicable sabotage that nature inflicted upon itself, had also come to haunt her. She felt almost unbearable guilt over the cost of her escape – a government man had died as a result of her drug deal. There was no doubt that many others too, taking the same stock of contaminated drugs, had died because of her. Damo had got the bar but he deserved it. He sent her a postcard from time to time.

As for Bellingham the traitor, he was surely dead by now of gout or a heart attack or syphilis.

A deep nihilism settled in her soul. Her counsellor told her that she had been depressed for years over some old loss: her mother, her dog, something. Then she got pregnant again and her anomie appeared to lift.

As time went by, Krista came to appreciate Amiel's qualities, which he seemed to have acquired after their separation ten years previously. Her husband now knew how to make love to her. He knew how to cook, how to keep house. He knew how to talk to her about film. He knew when she cried what she was crying for. They never talked about Dublin.

Amiel could delight her with a quicksilver tongue and delicate fingers and certain electrical appliances. He spoke perfect French to her in bed. It was corny but how flattering to be told she was beautiful in a language she found endlessly erotic and mysterious. What she liked most about him was that he was good with Louisa, taking her schooling seriously and picking her up from her classes in the evenings, bringing her down to the facilities house for a visit before dinner.

Amiel. The name sounded like that of an angel. If in heaven an angel is nobody in particular, she was lucky to have this one here where he stood out and was all hers.

The only things Krista didn't like in her husband were his middle-aged corpulence, his nailbiting habit and his breathing at night. In bed, when she was trying to sleep, he would often keep her awake with a jagged snore that, she imagined, sounded like a narwhal, the unicorn of the sea. Every time she felt a twinge of disgust at his deficiencies, she reminded herself that Amiel was good with her daughter and that mattered above all else.

Among their favourite ways to kill a Sunday afternoon was taking a picnic in the Jardins. You might see a Japanese group, wearing encounter suits because they'd heard so much about the U.V., here to visit the home of The Come Along Ponds. You might even spot an English couple, happily wandering. You would never see the Irish.

Up on the observation deck, Krista watched the tourists taking movies of Sacré-Coeur. Others stared without cameras in the direction of Chartres. It was time to come down. She had taken this day to herself, time out from her job at the Institute canteen, and her alone time was nearly done.

Krista waited for the elevator. She remembered coming to the Tower for the first time, five years before. Eiffel's room had been the same, but the lifelessness of the mannequins had disconcerted her. They looked like what they were: echoes in time. They had reminded her of Raimi. Ever since her escape, she had a recurring dream of her old lover on the cross, a profane negative of her religious orgasmic fantasies.

The elevator arrived. A guard held the rope aside. One of these days, Krista told herself, I'll get around to seeing the Mona Lisa.

Heading for ground level Krista became overwhelmed by voices in her head – the thoughts of her fellow passengers, which she was convinced she could hear. She was sure that the fat man in the Guggenheim Bilbao T-shirt was starving for pasta. The man behind her, whom she couldn't see but knew was there, played the Goldberg Variations in his mind. The woman to her left with the pearl-handled clasp-bag was looking forward to *soixante-neuf* in about one hour, with a burly man who sold dirty Victorian pictures. Krista had seen him before on the quays, this pornographer, and his serio prints of women dressed in the fashion of late nineteenth-century London, but with cutaway sections in which foetuses nestled, heads facing south. Krista had once been unfaithful to Amiel with an office worker she had met while browsing these images. It had meant nothing, and she never kept in touch with her. The memory of it now amused her.

The elevator soughed to a stop and the doors hissed open. Krista thought again of Raimi. He would have made a good father, probably, but she had never been entirely sure of him in that regard.

She wondered what Louisa was getting up to in school. English as a foreign language, perhaps.

Back on the streets, Krista spent the rest of the afternoon wandering in and out of bookshops. In Barnes, Noble, Shakespeare & Co., she found a copy of *102 H-Bombs* by Thomas M. Disch. It had been one of Raimi's favourites in his childhood, his lonely orphaned youth, though he had never read a book during their time together. She took it to the counter and bought it. The American bookseller imprinted the frontispiece with the famous rubber stamp of the shop, and bid her good day.

In the throng of shoppers on the Boulevard Palance near Notre Dame, Krista thought of preparing dinner for herself, Amiel and Louisa then remembered that this was her day off. Instead she would join them at the facilities house and go to a restaurant before Amiel had to return to work. There was bound to be a table at McDo's.

Amiel kissed their blonde, gamine daughter on the forehead and let her down off his knee. He went over to meet Krista before she got half way across the floor. They enfolded tenderly.

Louisa jumped up now, grabbing at Krista's arm, shouting 'Maman, maman!'

'Just a second'. Krista frowned at her daughter. She was enjoying her small moment with her husband.

On the console where Amiel had been working, the screen showed a photorealistic Woody Allen, frozen in a familiar pose: hands out in pathetic enquiry, eyes wide in bewilderment behind his trademark spectacles.

'Krista', Amiel whispered. 'Did you have a good day?'

'I went up the Eiffel Tower', she said. 'Saw all of Paris'.

'You sound as if you were bored'.

Louisa tugged at the hem of Krista's skirt.

'No. I'm always impressed with the view. Then', she nibbled his ear and drew back. 'Then I wandered around some bookshops and found a book Raimi used to like. It was his anniversary on Friday'.

'Raimi'. Amiel let her go.

Krista shook her head.

'How is my little angel?' She took Louisa up into her arms and kissed her. 'How was your day at school?'

'It was good?' Louisa said.

'That's right', said Krista. 'It was good'.

The McDo on the Champs Elysées was Krista's favourite. It was four flights above a gallery and the climb up the stairs always made sure of your hunger. The oil paintings on which the menus were painted in white letters, seemed to be actual Vermeers.

She liked their seats: original Louis XIV with the Golden Arches embroidered in the fabric. There was something very modern about that.

Minutes after she arrived with her family a waiter approached to take their orders. An elegant and elderly man, he sniffed at them before speaking.

'Madame'.

Krista picked up the menu, scanned it quickly. 'I'll have the Fondants de Poisson au Beurre de Citron. And the Magrets de Canard aux Poires'. She was pleased with her pronunciation. The waiter did not correct her.

'Monsieur?'

'Je voudrais Petits Farcis Niçois', Amiel said. 'Et les Escalopes de Saumon Gigondas'.

'Oui, monsieur'. The waiter tapped in his pad. 'Bien. Mademoiselle?'

Louisa smiled. 'Je voudrais un Big Mac et des frites'.

'Un moment', Krista said to the waiter, and put her hand up. 'Louisa, you can't order that'.

'Bof!'

The waiter suppressed a laugh at the girl's tiny joke.

'Ok mother', Louisa said. 'Salade Hermine, et Éstouffade de Boeuf Provençale'.

Krista drew her hand away. 'That's better!'

The waiter sighed a little too theatrically for Krista's taste.

'Isn't that a little heavy?' Amiel asked and sighed when no one answered.

'Très bien, mademoiselle. Du vin?' The waiter winked at the girl.

'Non!' Krista said. 'Water for the table. Pour trois'.

The waiter sniffed again and withdrew.

'You really shouldn't tell her what to order', Amiel said.

'I'm only trying to broaden her appreciation of cuisine'. Krista was properly miffed. It was vulgar to order the Big Mac and Louisa knew it.

The waiter returned with a bottle of Montpelier water.

The video wall lit up with a flicker and a movie began in a square of light. The sound was off but Krista recognised the film from the enormous grey bell tolling in silence and swinging towards the viewer. A title appeared: *Liberty Films Presents.*

'Shit!' she snapped. 'Louisa, don't look'.

The waiter unscrewed the bottle and started to pour into their glasses.

A title card replaced the bell with a still-frame illustration of two people in a horse-drawn buggy.

Amiel touched Krista's arm. 'Don't look at what?'

A page turned to reveal the next card: *Frank Capra's 'It's A Wonderful Life'. An RKO Radio Release.*

'Monsieur! Pardon, Monsieur', Krista began.

The waiter cocked an eyebrow and waited for her to continue. When she didn't, he set the bottle down, bowed slightly and departed.

The page on screen flipped over to reveal another. *Starring James Stewart.*

'Leave it, Krista'. Amiel said.

'Don't shout at me'. Krista put her hands over her ears.

Amiel huffed.

More pages flipped – the opening credits, all handwritten beautifully.

'Krista!'

'Maman, what's wrong?'

'Le film! Ce n'est pas for children!' Krista dropped her hands and hid them under the table.

'Don't be absurd', Amiel said.

Louisa shrugged. 'Maman, don't be absurd!'

'What the hell is wrong with you?' Amiel frowned at Krista. 'It's only a film'.

Krista could not look at the screen. She could not look. For distraction she focused on a fractured stab of acousmatic noise that now broke in the air outside. At first it sounded huge and empty, an explosion to which neither Amiel nor Louisa reacted.

On the screen, snow fell on a sign: YOU ARE NOW IN BEDFORD FALLS.

'I want to see what's making that din', she said. Her husband and child seemed barely to notice when Krista got up and went to the window.

The noise resolved into a wail that resonated like a siren, almost *musique concrète* – stuttering at first then echoing off the walls of buildings, feeding back on itself in layers as if it were an experiment. Krista tried to spot the source.

This was the hour when the gendarmerie came out, prowling in their prowl-cars, clearing up the homeless, gathering the immigrants, disinfecting Haussmann's blessed boulevards of strays, making the thoroughfares safe for the nouvelles vagabonds, the silicon mendicants who flocked here in their thousands. Krista flew out, describing an arc through that tunnel of distortion, escaping once again into Paris, the city of light.

About the Author

Patrick Chapman was born in 1968. His other books are the poetry collections *Jazztown* (1991), *The New Pornography* (1996), *Breaking Hearts and Traffic Lights* (2007), *A Shopping Mall on Mars* (2008), *The Darwin Vampires* (2010), and *A Promiscuity of Spines: New & Selected Poems* (2012); and the story collection *The Wow Signal* (2007). He has also written a *Doctor Who* audio adventure, *Fear of the Daleks* (2007); the award-winning short film *Burning the Bed,* starring Gina McKee and Aidan Gillen (2003); and episodes for the children's animated television shows *Garth & Bev* (2010) and *Wildernuts* (2013). With Philip Casey he founded the Irish Literary Revival website. With Dimitra Xidous he founded and edits the online poetry quarterly *The Pickled Body*. Chapman has been a finalist twice in the Hennessy Literary Awards and once for a *Naugatuck River Review* Narrative Poetry Award. He won first prize for a story in the *Cinescape* Genre Literary Competition. In 2010 his work was nominated for a Pushcart Prize. He lives in Dublin.